DEATH by PARKING

BOOK ONE

The Laundry

The Phantom

The Rendezvous

JVH

Los Angeles, CA

Death by Parking Book One

www.DeathByParking.com

Printed in the United States of America

Book design: Carla Green, claritydesignworks.com

ISBN: 978-0-9989033-0-9 print
ISBN-13: 978-0-9989033-1-6 ebook

There seems to be a requirement to dedicate books to someone. It's usually a friend, lover, mentor, someone who made this book 'possible.' As this is the first of a long series, I think the best dedication is to the muse, or in this case, muses.

Death by Parking is dedicated to those really good writers who crafted mysteries over the years. Those who taught by doing, who wrote for the love of the genre. Thanks to Dashiell Hammett, Raymond Chandler, and Robert B. Parker. I hope you can see just a slice of Spenser, Marlow, and Spade in Paul Manning.

Episode One

The Laundry

1

He Has a Gun

A ringing in the distance stirred me from a deep sleep. It took a moment before I could determine whether it was the phone or the door. It was the phone. It was still ringing after I checked the time, 7 AM, and I padded to the kitchen to silence it.

"Manning," I muttered. I don't do very well before my second cup of coffee.

"Paul Manning, the detective?" replied a silky soft voice. It was just too nice a voice for 7 AM. But then, who am I to argue with a voice like that, at any time?

"Yeah," I answered. It wasn't difficult affecting my surly, "who the hell are you" attitude after the amount of alcohol I had consumed the night before.

"This is Betty Beeson. I work for AB Parking in Hollywood. I'm in a lot of trouble and need your help." Her voice began to quaver and I knew at any moment she would start to sob. I can't stand a dame that cries, particularly one I haven't met. I decided to be a bit nicer. That usually isn't difficult for me with beautiful women, but in this case, who knew?

"Calm down, take a deep breath, and tell me why you called," I purred. My bobcat had become a kitten.

It spilled out of her like champagne from a tipped crystal flute. "I am the night manager at our garage on Hollywood and Vine. My shift ends at eight. I counted the money and it was short. I didn't steal it, Mr. Manning, really, I didn't. But when my boss finds out, he'll fire me. I need this job. I called my friend Shirley and she said to call you."

Shirley? The only Shirley I knew was the building manager at the Argyle Building on Vine. She and I had a thing going for a few months last year. We parted on good terms and she continues to drop by from time to time when she's lonely. But I digress.

Then it came together, a wonder in my condition. The Argyle was at Hollywood and Vine, AB ran the parking concession. It was a new building and had, in addition to the usual parking lot next door, a garage under the building for tenants, visitors and VIPs. There was an upscale hotel on the upper floors, the Cinegrill on the main floor, with offices in the rest. I wasn't aware that the building kept its parking open all night, but with all that activity, it made sense.

"Can you come right down?" she continued. "I need to have someone here when my boss gets in. He has a temper. He usually doesn't arrive until about ten. I'm going to wait for him because of the shortage. I'd feel much better if you were here."

Hell, business was slow. I had nothing better to do. Who knows? Maybe I could help her out and then play Anthony to her Cleopatra. "I will be there by nine-thirty." She said thanks and goodbye.

I put an extra spoonful of coffee in the coffeepot that morning. I like it strong. Then as it perked and that memorable smell began to fill the house, I opened the windows so it could mingle with the fresh morning air.

I was renting (well, really house-sitting) a bungalow just off Mulholland Drive, up the hill from Sunset. It was small but suited my needs. I took the coffee out on my porch and had my first smoke of the day.

I could see the city spread out below. It was July and going to be a hot one. Already a light layer of smog covered the LA basin. It was like a painting hung behind a bar for decades, familiar, yellowed with nicotine, but an old friend nevertheless.

That seven-AM phone call. Something didn't quite ring true. The story was too pat. Why didn't she call the cops? Was there something more to this? I thought I might go into the office a little early to find out what I could on AB Parking and our Miss Beeson.

As I walked out the door I grabbed my suit jacket and my gun. I carry a Colt Detective in a standard inside the belt holster. I don't plan for gun battles, but the Colt is perfect for close encounters. It fits well under my jacket and doesn't ruin the cut.

When you live in LA you drive a convertible. Mine is a 1955, white-over-red Pontiac Star Chief. With this weather you can leave it parked outside with the top down. That way I can hop into the driver's seat and impress the hell out of the neighbors, and hopefully not break my neck. I survived my death-defying leap this morning.

My office is only two blocks away from the Argyle, next to the Egyptian Theatre. I parked in the lot next-door and let myself in the side door. It opened onto the marble lobby. The Egyptian theme was carried over from the theater. You know, tall columns, palm trees, a pyramid or two and a small Sphinx guarding a waterfall. It was a bit fancy for my taste but the location was great and the price was right.

My exercise for the day was skipping the elevator and taking the stairs. Four flights was easy. Plus, the raised heart rate helped clear out the leftover alcohol from last night. My office was next to the stairs. The sign on the frosted glass read, "Paul Manning, Investigations." That sign was the fanciest part of the office. There were just two rooms. One was a reception area with a couple of chairs and small table, where I could make perspective clients wait until they got nervous. The other was my office, with a desk, file, two chairs, and a closet. A sink sat in one corner. Someday I am going to get a rubber plant.

I picked up my mail from the floor and stepped into my office. Seated at my desk, I lit a smoke. I remembered an article in the LA Examiner saying AB Parking was one of the many parking companies that sprung up after the war. Seems the founder, Art Ball, had come back from Germany with a few bucks and noticed that everyone in LA had a car and no place to park. He bought a couple of vacant lots and started charging a dime a day to park. Now, a dozen years later the price was up to a quarter and he lived in a big house in the canyon. His sign with the word, "Parking," and a stylized arrow was all over town. He bought or leased every available vacant lot and parked cars there. Now he had expanded his business to running parking for other companies, like the Argyle Building.

I gave Shirley a call and after some cooing and idle chitchat, I asked her about Betty.

"She's a nice girl, just in from Iowa," reported Shirley, "Like everyone else except me she wants to be a star, but needs to eat. I knew AB had the opening downstairs and recommended her. It worked out well since she used to work for her father who's an accountant. She lives in a room off Orange Grove." Actually, Shirley could be a star. She is a looker. Just hadn't sat on the right stool at Schwab's.

It was 9:20 so I walked the two blocks to the Argyle. The day was hot and the brim of my hat was getting damp. The parking entrance was on Vine. I walked down the ramp and asked the kid in the booth to point out the parking office. The garage was cool and it felt good to take off the hat. As I neared the office, I heard a scream…

2

My Second Body of the Day

I pulled my gun and ran to the door of the parking office. The door was ajar. I pushed it open and went in, gun first. It was a small office with another door that led, I assumed, into the rest of the building. There were a couple of desks, an adding machine, and a safe in the corner. A rubber plant stood next to the door.

Oh, yeah, on the floor was a pool of blood, and beside it, the source of the blood. The body wasn't moving, and the blood came from a knife wound in the chest. My carefully honed detective skills told me it was a knife wound since the knife was still stuck in the body. My years of experience also told me I didn't need my gun.

I glanced through the other door and saw the hall was clear. No suspect running away. But that scream was real enough.

The man was in his 30s, and wearing a suit and tie. I checked his pulse, found he had none. His wallet was in his inside jacket pocket. It inadvertently fell out into my hand when I reached for it. The ID said he was Gilberto Quintana. His business cards were in the wallet, too. They indicated that he was a manager for AB Parking.

Time to do the right thing. I called the police.

I had left the force about ten years ago. There was this misunderstanding between me and a suspect. I misunderstood him a little too hard and although my Sergeant tried to cover it up, the LA Times was on the warpath at that time over police brutality and I got the ax. I never had any animosity for the LAPD. I just didn't do well in that structured environment.

When I left the force I went to work for the Bel Air Patrol, a private police force that guarded all the movie stars and millionaires in Beverly Hills and Bel Air. Captain Hankins, former Beverly Hills Police Chief of Detectives, now in charge of the patrol, let me join him on some "informal" investigations to learn my trade. After five years of cleaning up after prima donnas, I went out on my own.

I didn't dial 911. I instead called the back line at the Hollywood cop shop. I figured my ex-partner would be at the desk. I was right.

"Vose," he said. Bill Vose was a good guy. I might need a friend here as I was the first on the scene and I didn't see any witnesses around to back up whatever version of the truth I might give.

"Bill, it's Paul Manning here. I'm in the parking office at the Argyle Building. There's a stiff on the floor that just bled out."

"Hold it a sec," he interrupted. I heard some mumbling in the background. "Ok, what else can you tell me? The uniforms are on the way."

"Not much," I said. "I came over to meet a gal I spoke to on the phone, walked in and found this guy on the floor."

"Yeah, right, Manning. You never just walk in and find a body. There's more to it than that. Stay there, I'll be right over."

I could hear the sirens approaching. The cops drove right into the garage. I replaced the wallet and waited for them. Two uniforms ran in with guns drawn. I thought for a minute I was in a Laurel and Hardy movie. One was tall and thin, the other short and fat.

"Down on the floor," the fat one said.

"Aw, come on, guys, I don't want to mess up the suit. Might get blood on it. I called Sergeant Vose. He's on his way."

"Well…" said the thin one – his name was Cooper (maybe it was a western, not a comedy). "Just turn around and keep your hands where we can see them."

After some discussion, we decided the wise thing to do was to move our little group outside the door and wait for Vose. Five minutes later he showed up with some guys from the crime lab.

"Anything else you want to tell me?" he said. He wasn't happy.

"What do you mean, Bill?" I flashed a million-dollar smile. Bill Vose was about five years my senior. He was a career cop and a good one. I could describe him but instead, just imagine all the lovable, curmudgeonly cops you have ever known, and that was Bill. His suit, however, unlike most cops', fit properly (his wife made sure of that). And he didn't have the look of a curmudgeon. He was 6' 2" and 205 pounds. He worked out. The girls loved him. But he loved his wife.

"What about the blonde? What about the scream? Is the dead guy the manager?" Wow, he was good. He hadn't been there five minutes and knew as much as I did. I glanced over at the kid from the parking booth. He had a sheepish grin.

I told Bill the story from the beginning, leaving out just enough not to convict Betty. He told me not to leave town. Nope—I was in a detective movie.

I went to the pay phone on the wall in the garage and called Shirley, who had recommended Betty for the job, and she gave me Betty's address. Maybe I could beat Vose there and find out what was going on.

The place was a rooming house on Orange Grove, a couple of blocks from the Argyle. It was called the Orange Blossom Arms. It was clean enough, and run by a woman named Marlene Crowley, who could best be described as handsome.

Let's just say she shopped at plus-size stores and came across like a center for the LA Rams. There was no way I was getting past her. Period.

"Who the hell do you think you are, barging in here and asking about Betty? I run a respectable place where girls can feel safe from guys like you. And don't try using any lines on me. I've heard them all."

Obviously my signature smile wouldn't help either, so I tried the last tool in my kit. The truth.

"I got a call from Betty telling me she was in trouble. When I got to her office she wasn't there but the police were. I came here to help her." I could see Marlene was beginning to thaw.

"Well, I'll tell you what. I'll go with you. I know she's home, saw her come in about 15 minutes before you. But if she doesn't know you, buster, you'll wish you never entered the Blossom." I believed her.

Betty's place was in the back on the first floor. Marlene knocked, with no answer. "Betty, it's Marlene." Still no answer. I was preparing to kick down the door when Marlene held up her hand. She gave me a look that would have stopped a clock, took out her passkey, and unlocked the door.

The room looked like a china shop just after the bull left. Clothes were strewn everywhere, the mattress was upended, drawers open. I walked to the bathroom and stopped. There on the floor was my second body of the day…

3

I Yelled, He Fired

It was a good-looking blonde. The scream from behind me told me it was Betty. Damn, sometimes things just don't go right.

As I bent closer I heard a soft moan. It was coming from Betty. Maybe sometimes things do go right. Marlene, embarrassed by her scream, was already reaching for the phone. Help was on the way.

Betty began to stir and I checked her out as best I could. Except for a goose egg on her head, she seemed OK. I picked her up. Marlene had straightened the mattress and watched my every move as I laid her on the bed. She couldn't have weighed more than 110 pounds. Marlene placed a cool towel on her head. Her eyes opened, the most beautiful blue pools I had ever seen. Oh, Betty, where have you been all my life?

"It's, OK, sweetheart, you are going to be all right," I murmured. I'm not any better with recovering blondes than I am with crying ones.

"Who are you?" she asked.

"Paul Manning. I dropped by when you didn't keep your appointment at the garage."

"Oh, yes....Gilberto—is he...?"

"Dead? Yes. He has nothing on a doornail. Do you feel up to talking about it?" Maybe I could get some information before the police arrived.

"Sure," she said. "We Midwestern girls have hard heads. About 9:30 I went to the ladies room and when I returned I found Gilberto. I guess I panicked. I ran out of the office, up the stairs and came here. When I walked in, there was a man going through my things. I surprised him, we struggled, and he hit me on the head. That's it."

It was my second dose of "a little too pat" from my Midwestern, hardheaded blonde. First the story on the phone that got me involved, then this.

"What was he looking for?" I asked.

"I…I don't know. I couldn't imagine. I don't have anything of value," she said.

"Come on, honey, I don't have all day. My buddy Bill Vose, that's *Sergeant* Bill Vose, from the LAPD is going to be here any minute and he's not going to buy your story any more than I do. If I am going to help you I need to know the truth. Once you are booked, and you will be booked, at least for Quintana's murder, it will be more difficult to talk."

"But…I didn't kill Gilberto. I found the body," she said.

"Yeah, but what about your fingerprints on the knife?" said I.

"Well, I might have touched the knife when I found him," she responded.

"See how easy it is? I didn't know your prints were on the knife. I just said they were and you fell for it. You're in deep, kiddo. Now let's hear it, all of it."

"OK. I have been working for AB Parking for about six months. I noticed some substantial irregularities in the way money is handled. There are parking permits 'off the books' and the daily cash doesn't add up. And there are other problems; I have been keeping a record of all the issues. I was going to take it to the owner, but then I didn't know if he was involved.

"Yesterday, Larry, the cashier, saw me working on my book. I was pretty sure that he was in on the scam, although I wasn't sure to what extent. I was afraid he might tell Gilberto, so I called my friend Shirley and she told me to call you."

"Why didn't you call the police?" I asked.

"Well, I'm new to this business and I didn't know how much of what I found was routine, and how much theft. And I didn't know whether or not the owner was involved. I mean, if he was, then he was stealing from himself and besides, why would the police care about his bookkeeping practices?

"Gilberto got there early. He was furious. He asked me to see my book. I told him that I didn't have it there at the office, it was at home. He made a phone call, spoke to someone in Spanish, and then started yelling at me. He called me names and slapped me. Then he pulled out this knife and started toward me. I backed up toward the door. He tripped over the rubber plant and fell. When I turned him over, the knife was in his chest. I guess I touched it when I rolled him over. Then I came here."

Damn, I knew those rubber plants were useful but I never figured one to be a defender of beautiful women. I guess I didn't need one in my office, it had me.

The story was still hazy, but we were getting closer. I would leave it at that for now.

"What happened to the book?" I said.

"I gave it to Shirley last night for safekeeping. I didn't tell her what it was, I just asked her to hold it for me."

Now I had an excuse to drop by and see my old flame. Not that I needed one, but it never hurts. Even with a good attorney, Betty was going to be tied up with the police for the next few days. That gave me some time to run this thing down.

I could hear the cops rolling up outside.

"Here come the police. Don't say anything. I'll call my lawyer and have him meet you at the station. In the meantime,

I will sniff around and see what I can find out about our Mister Gilberto Quintana and Art Ball of AB Parking."

Vose walked in and I was back in the detective movie. No need to go through the dialogue. You could write it. It ended with "don't leave town." I left him arguing with the stalwart Marlene Crowley, in search of a phone more private than the one in Betty's room.

I decided to start at the top. Maybe I could find out something from the owner of AB, Mr. Art Ball.

I got his address from Shirley, and at the same time set up dinner with her. Might as well ask for the book and have fun at the same time.

Ball lived in one of the smaller houses in Bel Air. Most people think Beverly Hills is THE address in LA, but no, the really rich live in Bel Air, behind walls and gates, with their own 24-hour private police force. The house was right on the golf course, just off Stone Canyon Drive. It was about a block, if they had blocks in Bel Air, from the Bel Air Hotel. I had asked Shirley to meet me there for dinner. Good place to let a few movie stars have a look at me.

Typical of Bel Air homes, the place was gigantic. There was parking behind the open gate for 10 cars and the carport held a Jag and an MG. The guy liked British cars. There was an empty space and I assumed it held a Rolls. There were a couple of American cars parked over to the side. My guess: the hired help. A large fountain in the courtyard featured a woman with the water cascading over all the right places. You had to walk around the wet wonder to reach the front door.

The door was standing open. I pulled my gun and went in. The first thing I saw was a fellow in a butler's uniform with his hands raised, backing up toward me.

In front of him was a big guy with a gun. I yelled, he fired…

4

Taken for a Ride

Fortunately, this gunsel was not a good shot, or perhaps it was my manly detective-style shout that made him miss both the butler and me. Instead, the bullet added to the design of a large painting behind me. The picture was the size of half a wall, but it couldn't have cost much as it had no trees or horses.

I dove for cover; the butler fainted. Our shooter did the same (dove for cover). We exchanged a couple of shots, and I guess he knew he was out-gunned, so he took off through an open set of French doors. I ran to the front door and took a carefully aimed shot. I winged him in the leg, but it didn't slow him down. He fled down the fairway of the Bel Air Country Club and disappeared behind a sand trap.

Hearing a moan behind me, I turned to see the butler starting to come around. I helped him to a chair and asked him what happened. Jeeves—I kid you not, that was his name—began his story.

"I returned from shopping and helped the cook put away the groceries. I then came in to the study and found this guy going through Mr. Ball's desk. He saw me and pulled out his gun. That's when you showed up. Thanks for the help, but who are you, anyway?"

"I'm Paul Manning, private detective," I said. "I work for one of Mr. Ball's employees and came by to talk to him. I guess my timing was good. Is Mr. Ball at home?"

"I don't think so," said Jeeves. "He told me he was going out, and his car isn't in the carport where he usually leaves it."

At that moment, a man came in like he owned the place. Turned out he did.

"What's going on here?" he said. "Who are you? Why is the door open?" Jeeves introduced us and then told Ball the story.

"I guess I owe you a debt of gratitude, Manning," Ball said. He didn't seem too surprised that someone had been searching his house. I asked him about it.

"Well, I'd rather not discuss it with you until I find out who you are and why you are here. Today has been a busy day for my company. One of my managers is dead and another is under arrest. And I have no idea what's going on."

I brought him up to speed as best I could. I left out the part about Betty's notebook, which I would look at when I met Shirley at the Bel Air Hotel for dinner. I wanted to know what was worth killing for before I discussed it with anyone.

"Well, it seems that you are one step behind whoever is behind this. Why don't you have a drink and let me make a couple of calls. If you check out, we'll have a little chat."

Jeeves took me into the next room, a combination poolroom, library and bar. He joined me in the drink. Neither of us thought his boss would mind. It was just to settle his nerves, of course.

I have been a single-malt whisky man ever since a friend introduced me to the rich, smoky taste of an 18-year-old Macallan a number of years back. I have a collection of single malts at home and have grown to like Laphroaig. It's a perverse little whisky distilled on the Isle of Islay, off the west coast of Scotland. It tastes of the land of its creators—tough, rough, peaty, with just a hint of the sea. (Some people think it tastes like iodine, but they don't appreciate the nuances of the dark amber liquid.)

The familiar green bottle with the white label was on the shelf, and I helped myself to three fingers and a splash of spring water. (The water cuts the alcohol so it doesn't burn and ruin the flavor. It also releases the flavor buds in the whisky. A Scotsman taught me this trick. People who drink their whisky "straight" are simply wrong.)

I was savoring my first sip when Ball walked in, poured himself a wee dram of 12-year-old Talisker, and said, "Well, you are who you say you are. I called a friend at City Hall, and he referred me to a police detective named Vose. He said you were a pain in the butt, but that you were honest and usually did what you said you would do. That's good enough for me."

Good old Bill. Couldn't give a reference without adding that "pain in the butt." Oh, well, it had obviously impressed Ball.

"Vose also said he was on his way over, and if you were still here, you should wait. I mentioned the problem of the intruder, and Vose said he would take the report when he arrived."

Ball then went on to tell me that he'd had several recent inquiries into the possibility of selling his parking business. He wasn't interested, but the potential buyers were insistent. He was becoming concerned, because through his contacts, he had learned that the buyers had connections in Las Vegas and New Jersey. I kinda figured what that meant.

Ball asked if I would work for him and look into the matter. I told him I already had a client, but maybe we could share information as the case developed. He thought that was a great idea.

It was getting late. I was supposed to wait for Vose, but Shirley would be in the bar at the Bel Air Hotel. I wanted to see that notebook, and I wanted to see Shirley.

Ball agreed to tell Vose where I was and that if he needed me to come back, to call over to the hotel. It was only five minutes away.

As I drove over to the hotel, I reviewed the day:

Less than 11 hours ago, I got a phone call from Betty. She was scared, and I agreed to meet her. I found a dead body, which turned out to be her immediate supervisor, on the floor of her office in the parking garage at the Argyle Building in Hollywood. When I went to Betty's apartment, I found her out cold and the place ransacked. When she came to, she told me she had found suspicious accounting activity at the garage and had a notebook detailing the discrepancies. Betty had given the notebook to Shirley for safekeeping. Her boss—Gilberto Quintana—was harassing her about the notebook, came at her with a knife, tripped on a rubber plant, and fell on the thing. (Well, that was her story and she was sticking to it.) I then went to Ball's house and found a gorilla looking through his papers. After a shootout, he escaped and Ball told me that I'm now involved with some shady characters who drive black cars and take people on one-way rides.

Ah, what 11 hours can do.

At the Bel Air Hotel, I opted to park my own car, although the valets are probably better drivers than I am. As I walked across the parking lot, I saw Shirley standing at the valet station. She was chatting with an officer from my former employers: the private police force for the stars, the Bel Air Patrol.

The Bel Air Hotel is one of the swankiest spots in LA. It's located in Stone Canyon, in the heart of Bel Air. Imagine a California jungle with 75-year-old oaks and sycamores, cozy little red-tiled cottages scattered among them. Now add that the place charges four times what the best hotels in Beverly Hills charge, throw in a best-of-show French restaurant, include two employees for every guest; you get the idea.

I had about 100 yards to go to catch up with her when two guys came out of the darkness and said: "You Paul Manning?"

"Who wants to know?" I responded. I was good at this gangster repartee.

"Da boss wants to see you, NOW!" They took my gun, shoved me in the back seat of a big black car, and off we drove…

5

The Shock of My Life

I knew this wasn't the Bel Air welcome wagon. The first clue was the black bag over my head. I was pretty sure I would be OK since, if this was a "one-way" ride, they wouldn't bother with the bag.

I knew that Shirley and the Bel Air Patrolman she was talking to at the hotel saw the incident and hopefully would do something about it. In the meantime the two gorillas on either side of me limited my options. I just sat back and waited.

The ride wasn't long. After about ten minutes we came to a stop and I was "escorted," well, dragged might be a better word, out of the car and taken into a house. We walked down a long hall and through a couple of rooms and I was told to sit there. The former inmates of the LA Zoo (or was it the Palermo Zoo) remained, as did the hood.

A few minutes later someone came into the room. He sat down a few feet in front of me (probably behind a desk) and then surprised me. It wasn't a "he," but the voice I heard came from a woman. It was clear, sultry, and had a wonderful southern European accent. It was soft, like moonlight dancing on the Spanish steps in Rome. But it was also as dangerous as the growl of a she-wolf on the slopes of Mt. Etna.

"Welcome, Mr. Manning," she said. "Sorry for all the histrionics, but I needed to speak to you while keeping my identity unknown, for at least a while longer. You understand, don't you?"

"The phone would have served the same purpose and not made you guilty of kidnapping," I snapped.

"I don't like to use the phone. It's easier to get one's point across in person," she said, emphasizing the word "point."

"Let's keep this short and sweet. You are meddling where you're not welcome. You are above average in intelligence so you have probably surmised the identity of the group I represent."

At least she didn't dangle a participle. Must have learned English in school.

"My principals want no trouble, they just want to purchase a few businesses here in LA, and we would prefer that you and the police keep out of our business. Let me say that your health, and that of Miss Beeson's and Shirley Williams', will remain as it is if you keep to yourselves and out of my business with Art Ball."

I would have preferred her threat if it were had a few more veils. She was about as subtle as the garlic in a plate of pasta with prawns. She got up and walked out without waiting for an answer. I was back in the movies, but this time it had mob written all over it.

I was then asked to stand and escorted out of the room. It was back to the car and then we took a 15-minute drive. I was convinced it took 15 minutes because they wanted me to believe it was a long way from Bel Air. The car stopped and I was let out. They graciously left the black bag over my head.

I removed the bag and realized I was standing about a block from the Bel Air Hotel.

Before I could take a step, a Bel Air Patrol Car drove up with Shirley Williams and the Patrol's Chief Captain Art Hankins in the back seat. It was driven by a patrolman I knew from my sojourn with the outfit a few years back. His name was Jim Walsh. His Irish accent gave away his heritage, although he was born in Chicago, not County Cork.

"Betty and I gave chase after we saw you picked up at the Bel Air," he said. "But we lost you up on Casiano. I radioed the Captain and he said to go back and pick him up at East Gate. Then we alerted all the cars on patrol. We spotted you again about six blocks from here. Looked to us like they were just driving around to confuse you."

"Well, Manning, it's good to see you're OK," said Captain Hankins. "We were a little concerned."

Captain Hankins was a former Chief of Detectives at the Beverly Hills PD. Upon his retirement, he was hired by the fine citizens of Bel Air to run their private police department, and hired me when I got sideways with the LAPD. He took an interest in me and taught me the detective business. Many of the "landed gentry," including a large number of "A-list" stars, live in Bel Air and use the patrol to wash their dirty laundry. Although he's the Chief of this force, he went by his Beverly Hills title, Captain.

It was the Captain and Jim, by the way, that picked up a certain singer's kidnapped son (the singer was also the board chairman) walking along the street after his release. He hid junior in his car's trunk to get by the reporters outside dad's gate. Papa showed his appreciation to Jim and the Captain in the usual way.

"We ran the plate," the Captain said. "It was stolen from a '53 Ford pickup. Had no relationship to that mob wagon you were in. What's going on, Paul?"

Shirley jumped out and gave me a hug. She usually handles things like this pretty well. Guess that's what I lo…lo...lo…like about her. Just can't quite say the "l" word, but if I ever do, Shirley most likely will be the recipient. Our relationship was great, but neither of us was ready to settle down. We both saw other people, but always seemed to get back together.

"Chief, I'll come by tomorrow and fill you in, but now Shirley and I have a dinner reservation. Would you like to join us?"

The Chief demurred. I knew he would, and if he hadn't, we would have had words later. Jim dropped us off at the Bel Air and the evening interruptus continued.

We walked across the short bridge to the lobby building. The lobby is lined with pictures of some of the former guests, including almost every movie star you ever heard of, a Prince (before he ascended the throne), and some junior senator from Mass who was there on his honeymoon. He had married a socialite named Bouvier and picked this spot to hide from the limelight. Their picture was right next to that new bombshell that was taking Hollywood by storm, Marilyn Monroe.

Entering the bar was like stepping in to a 19th century English Gentlemen's Club. It was dark with mahogany paneling, a piano, soft leather sofas all around, a large crackling fire (even when it was 100 outside) and a bar man who knew what you wanted without your having to tell him, as long as you had been there at least once.

"Hi, Mr Manning, got some 18-year-old Laphroig back here. That OK? And a martini-up with two olives, for Miss Williams." I nodded and we sat on a nearby sofa. He came with the drinks, along with a small crystal pitcher of spring water for me. He knew how single-malt whisky should be served.

I had just picked up the glass and was about to propose a toast to Shirley, and a little notebook, when I heard a voice that sounded exactly like moonlight on the Spanish steps. I turned around and got the shock of my life…

6

Say Goodbye to the Convertible

She was not only beautiful, but also recognizable. No wonder I had a hood over my head when we last met.

She was an up-and-coming, below-the-title star who it was rumored dated Howard Hughes. I don't know whether it was before, during, or after Ava Gardner, or was it Katherine Hepburn, Ginger Rogers, Terry Moore, Lana Turner, or his current wife, actress Jean Peters. Well, the guy did get around. I would have to check out her name and then find out if she was still on Hughes' A-list.

I turned back to Shirley who was listening to the jazz from the piano, but began to wonder about the Hughes connection. I knew that he was involved with the new intelligence operation of the US Government called the Central Intelligence Agency. He was also close to the FBI and J. Edgar Hoover.

His dislike for the Kennedy Family and Papa Joe in particular was no secret. Howard had shafted Joe on a movie deal and Joe didn't like to be shafted. Joe had a lot of money and having him as an enemy could be a problem. Blood was bad between those two.

Joe Kennedy was financing his number-two son, Jack, that junior senator from Mass, in a run for president. Number-one son was killed during the war. Howard could cause some problems for Joe. I wondered if Joe knew that Howard had squired Ava around town. Maybe the well-known relationship between Joe and Ava was intended to send a message to Howard.

Perhaps the fact that Bobby Kennedy, son number-three, was chief counsel for the senate rackets committee also caused old Howard some pain. There was certainly a relationship between the CIA, the Mob, the FBI, and Hughes. Who knows, I may have found the connection right there on the voice from the Spanish steps.

Sorry about the history lesson, I do get carried away…

What in the heck did the Mob, Howard Hughes, the CIA, and J Edgar Hoover have to do with the takeover of a parking operation in Los Angeles. Maybe the answer lay in that little book I could see peeking out of Shirley's handbag.

I was about to ask Shirley for the book but then, remembering the person sitting just one chair away, I thought better of it. Perhaps that was a request better done in private.

The song ended and Shirley looked over my shoulder and whispered, "This is so exciting, there are movie actors and actresses all over the place. Heck, that's Maria LaFlonza sitting right next to you."

I guess the fact that my eyebrows were practically aligned with my hairline signaled something to Shirley, so she added: "You know, she was in that picture a couple of years ago with Ingrid Bergman, Stromboli. You remember, we went to it, it had subtitles."

Sure, I remembered. I think I fell asleep five minutes into the first reel. However, I did recall one thing, it was produced by RKO, and that was after Hughes stole the business from Joe Kennedy. The plot thickens. I was certainly in the movies now.

We finished our drinks and went on to dinner. It's an elegant restaurant, the Bel Air, with great food and great wine, plus this evening the French doors were open and the scent of the flowers along Stone Canyon brook was intoxicating. After dinner, I drove Betty home.

Both of us were stressed from the long day so we said goodnight on the porch. Betty handed me the notebook and I went home.

I glanced through the book and saw that it contained a series of numbers, dates, and dollar amounts. It would take more than a cursory reading it to figure it out. I would need help. I also knew that the book wasn't safe as long as it was with me.

I called a friend (hopefully, she would remain a friend after I called her at 11 PM) and asked for her assistance.

Mary Root was one of the best stenographers in the city. She was fast and extremely accurate, and I needed a copy of the book tonight. She wasn't happy, but when I noted that the fee, in addition to the usual $50 she charged, would be dinner, dancing, and a show in Hollywood, a smile crept into her voice. She told me to come right over.

Within an hour she had copied the entire notebook and with the help of good old carbon paper, I had two copies. I gave her the fifty and we set a date for the upcoming weekend for the rest of the payoff.

I then went to my office in Hollywood. By now it was after midnight, but the security guard let me in and I had the building to myself. I bound the notebook in brown paper, secured it with string, and addressed it to my landlord in Idaho. I put one of the copies in an envelope and addressed it to my post office box in Hollywood. I then set off for Terminal Annex, the main post office next to Union Station downtown. It was open 24 hours.

Only in LA. The building, which is really just a post office, was built in Spanish/Moroccan-style with two bell towers and tile splashed everywhere. It's across the street from Olvera street, the Mexican adobe area that was the beginning of the El Pueblo de Nuestra Señora la Reina de Los Ángeles del Río

Porciúncula. That's LA's complete name. To keep this missive from going on forever, I'll just call it LA.

The clerk told me the postage would be a dollar for the book and a dime for the envelope. I gave him a buck-ten and left the only clue I had in the secure hands of the US Government.

I went home with my copy and fell into bed.

The next morning dawned cool, as it often does in LA in the early summer. I looked out over the LA basin and saw nothing but layers of gray fog. It would burn off about 10 or so, but in the meantime, June gloom had definitely arrived. The folks at the beach would be lucky to see the sun at all.

I called my landlord and told her to expect a package from me and to hold it until I got back in touch. Then I decided to have breakfast at Ship's on La Cienega and decide what to do with the information contained in Betty's notebook.

As I started down the hill I noticed a big black car pull in behind me. It didn't look like it belonged in my neighborhood; in fact, it looked strangely familiar, like the one that gave me a lift the previous night.

Any sane person would have continued on with their daily chores, but sanity wasn't big in my family. I pulled a quick right on Coldwater Canyon and headed for Mulholland Drive. It's a twisty two-lane road that runs the length of the Santa Monica Mountains, from the Hollywood Bowl and the new Hollywood Freeway on the east, to the Pacific Coast Highway alongside the ocean. Parts of it weren't paved.

I figured my car being smaller and having a better driver could lose the mob wagon easily on the Drive's hairpin curves.

Mulholland Drive was named after William Mulholland, the father of water in Southern California. His idea was to take the water from the Eastern Sierra Nevada Mountains in the northern part of the state and bring it to LA. That water would then turn the San Fernando Valley from the desert it was in 1910, to the paradise it is today. What he neglected to tell the public was that he and his cronies had purchased most of the valley for pennies an acre and would sell it when the water started flowing for a hundred times that cost.

The road that bears his name had become a favorite spot for kids to park. It was dark and had a great view, particularly at night, although I'm not sure anyone was interested. As Groucho Marks said, the tulips (read that two lips) were always blooming at night up on Mulholland Drive.

I turned left toward the ocean and floored it. The Pontiac's V-8 responded and I began to leave my Sicilian friends in the dust. I was feeling pretty proud of myself as I accelerated and rounded a sharp curve. Dead ahead, not more than 100 feet, was a flagman and a construction crew. I downshifted, and started to slide sideways into the road-grader that blocked the road.

The flagman dove out of the way as I swept past at a good 60-miles-per-hour. There was no question that when I hit the grader there would be more than a slight bump.

At that moment everything seemed to go into slow motion. I hit the brakes and the car bucked, tossing me into the windshield. The last thing I remember was the gas tank of the grader not more than two feet away and the car sliding right toward it....

7

Shirley Storms Out

If this was heaven, I was glad I died. When I opened my eyes I saw the most beautiful angel dressed in white. Plus, she was stroking my chest with a sponge filled with warm water. Ah, what a life…or death.

When she saw my eyes open, she smiled and asked if I knew my name. Heck, didn't St. Peter have a list? But she was so pretty, how could I refuse. I told her I was the late Paul Manning, LA Private Eye. She laughed and asked what I was late for.

"You know, late, as in dead, passed on, stone cold," I said. She laughed again.

"You're not dead; you're in the City of Angels hospital. Actually, you're pretty lucky. No broken bones, only a slight concussion. It could have been a lot worse; when you came in, your clothes smelled like gasoline. I understand your car is a total wreck."

Suddenly it all came rushing back: the dead body, my beautiful client, the shootout in a Bel-Air mansion, being kidnapped by the Mob, and threatened by a woman with a voice that sounds like moonlight on the Spanish Steps in Rome. And all this over the proposed takeover of Art Ball's parking operation. Oh yes, and the notebook that Betty gave to my girlfriend, Shirley Williams, for safekeeping. Then there was that actress, plus Howard Hughes, JFK, the FBI, J. Edgar Hoover, the CIA, being chased by the Mob, and that road-grader on Mulholland Drive. Seemed clear to me now, despite the fuzzy thoughts.

I started to get up and a brass band went off in my head. The angel told me to rest, that she had finished the sponge bath and the doctor would be in to talk to me. I asked what day it was and found that I had only been out a few hours.

At least if I didn't move my head I could think about this case. Imagine, killing someone over a parking lot. It seemed absurd. But then Ball did live in Bel Air, so unless his daddy had bucks, there must be something to this parking. As for the Mob, why would they want a parking lot? What could be so interesting about dimes and quarters?

It all must revolve around Betty's notebook. I had sent the original to my landlord in Idaho for safekeeping but had a copy in my jacket. I wondered if it was still there. When the angel came back I asked about my personal effects. They were in a drawer at the bedside and sure enough, there was the notebook copy. It smelled a lot like gasoline.

"Your clothes were a lost cause. We had to toss them. We did keep everything in your pockets; you'll find it all in the drawer. Now get some rest. The doctor will be in later."

I leafed through the notebook. It was divided into days of the week, a page for each day. At the top of every page, below the date, were two five-digit numbers, and a three-digit number, like 15052—15451—225.

Then there were columns of numbers, each containing four rows.

15052	0800	1152	1
15053	0815	1500	1
15057	0815	0902	.25
15058	0820	0924	.50, and so on.

The last number was 15451.

And at the bottom of the page was a number circled, D=$725.

None of it made sense. I needed help to figure it out.

I picked up the phone and called Shirley. I thought she might be able to recommend someone who could decipher this. She said that the parking business was relatively new, but that Ball had taken her lot over from an old-timer that might help, "DC" McGuire. He had retired after running some parking lots in LA and in New York City.

I called "DC" and his wife answered. He would call me back when he returned from the golf course that afternoon. Then the Angel came in and forced a pill down me. I woke up six hours later with the phone ringing.

"This is DC.," said the person at the other end of the line. "I understand you want to talk parking." I explained that I was indisposed at the moment, and he volunteered to come by the hospital that afternoon. "I'm retired and have little to do except golf."

"DC" was still dressed in plus-fours, a fancy shirt, and knee socks when he arrived. He looked like he'd just stepped off the last green at the Olde Course in St. Andrews, not the Rancho Park Golf Course in West LA.

"I ran the auditing department for a large parking outfit in New York," he told me. "Then they sent me to LA to solve some problems here. I liked it and stayed."

I told him what had happened, and showed him the notebook. I had no choice. It was literally just numbers to me, but maybe this retired parking pro could sort it out. He looked at the book for about five minutes and started to laugh. "I would have to see the lot and look at the books there to be sure," he said between chuckles, "but I think you have a laundry on your hands."

"Huh? I didn't see anything that looked like a laundry at the lot. Just a bunch of cars and—"

"No, not that kind of laundry, a money laundry. Someone is turning dirty cash into legit funds, and using the parking lot to do it. See, if you make a bunch of money illegally on prostitution or running a gambling parlor, you have a lot of folding green, but how can you use it. People would get suspicious if you showed up to buy a house with $25,000 in cash. And you can't just deposit it in the bank; the Feds would begin to wonder about the source of your income. Parking is a cash business. No one will ever make you account for all the money. There's no inventory to list and track, so unless you are knowledgeable about the parking business, there is no way to prove just how much money is collected on any given day.

"In parking, you are renting space by time. Who knows how many cars come and go and how long they stay? So although you actually collect, say, $225 on a given day, who says you can't put $750 or $1000 in the bank. At that moment, the additional $525 or $775, which may be the result of a bank robbery or numbers running, becomes perfectly legitimate. You pay your taxes, and buy your house, or limo, or whatever."

"But how could laundering $500 or $750 a day mean much to a group the size of the mob?" I asked.

"Well, if you have 50 lots at $500 a day, the numbers mount up fast. By the way, whoever kept these figures must have had a lot of time on their hands and a grasp of accounting." I immediately thought of Betty's work hours on the night shift and her accountant father in Iowa. "I wish I had that person working for me. We could have uncovered a lot of theft," he added.

My head was spinning and it wasn't from the run-in with the road-grader. It still didn't make sense. If money was being laundered in Ball's parking lots, and the local Mafia was involved, wouldn't they have cut a deal BEFORE they started moving money through the books? Or maybe they thought they had a deal but my single-malt-scotch-loving friend, Art Ball, had reneged on the deal. Maybe he didn't know the rules of the game these folks played.

I needed more details and the place to get them was Betty. The problem was that I didn't know what questions to ask. I had the fountain of all parking knowledge right in front of me. Maybe it was time to forge a stronger relationship. Golfers drink. Retired folks who play golf drink a lot.

I made an appointment to meet "DC" for cocktails at the nineteenth hole at Rancho Park the next afternoon. The doctor dropped in just before "DC's" arrival and told me I would be released tomorrow morning. He wanted to keep an eye on me overnight. The rest would do me good, he said. And I could get better acquainted with my new guardian angel.

She was going off-shift and dropped in to chat. Turns out her name was Mary. She sat on the bed and was holding my hand and saying all the nice things nurses know how to say when my girlfriend Shirley walked through the door with a vase of flowers.

Now Shirley and I don't have a fully committed relationship; however, she is definitely more committed than I. Her smile turned to stone in an instant and with a voice that could freeze water said, "Well, glad to see you are feeling better." She tossed the flowers on the bed and stormed out.

8

They Have Shirley

Shirley and I have a long history and it's a good one. But I decided to sit back and enjoy the present company, since it was obvious I wasn't going to have any from Shirley until she cooled off. The main problem was that the water from the vase was soaking through the blanket and my feet were getting wet.

Mary quickly grabbed the vase before all the water spilled out and set it on the table next to the bed.

"Sorry," she said, "I guess you are taken," and she also walked out.

Boy, how quickly it can all go to hell. Nothing to do now but sleep off the pain from my accident, then prepare for the meeting with "DC" and Betty.

The next morning I was feeling almost well. I called my lawyer, the insurance company and then rented a car. I would be looking for a new car but in the meantime the clunker from "Rent-a-Wreck" would have to do. I figured that my next move should be to contact my buddy at the LAPD, Bill Vose, and get an update on the status of my client, Betty. I thought this would be better done in person, since the last time I was scheduled to see Bill I stood him up, or rather, my kidnapping by the mob circumvented our meeting. After dropping by my house to get some clean clothes, I headed for downtown LA.

His office was in the newly opened Police Administration Building. Vose was at his desk muttering under his breath. "What's the problem?" I asked.

"It's about time you showed up, you are only 36 hours late for our little meeting in Bel Air. I understand you've been a bit busy. How's the head?"

I told Vose that I was fine and asked about my client.

"She will be released later today. That Philadelphia lawyer you hired knows her stuff. Plus, Betty's landlady is known by the DA's office as a straight-shooter and she vouched for her."

I knew that Marlene Crowley, the linebacker than runs the Orange Blossom Arms, would somehow reappear in this story. She nearly decked me when I tried to get to Betty's room after I found Gilberto Quintana, Betty's boss, in a pool of blood in her office at the parking garage. However, my silver tongue, and the truth, got us moving and we found Betty out cold on the floor of her bathroom. The police arrived and arrested Betty, but as I left, Marlene had Bill Vose in a verbal hammerlock and I knew he was going to rollover.

"You can probably take Betty with you when you leave," Vose added.

"Great. Now, what's been happening with the shootout in Bel Air and my timeout with the mob?"

"Oh, right, you haven't heard. Well, the fellow you winged running out of Art Ball's house in Bel Air turned up in Vegas with a bullet through his head; yours was in his hip. That's how we ID'ed him. Your previous activities have given us a record of the ballistics off your piece. No question, it was an execution. Definitely mob-related.

"As for the kidnappers, the car chasing you on Mulholland and its occupants weren't so lucky. When they rounded the curve and saw you slide into the road-grader, they went into a spin and wound up wrapped around an oak tree. No survivors. We compared the plate with the one we got from Captain

Hankins over at Bel Air and it matched, stolen from a '53 Ford Pickup. It seems you've developed a tendency to leave a string of bodies in your wake."

"Just talented, I guess," I said. "Thanks for the info. Where can I meet Betty?"

Vose called down to have Betty brought up. She looked good, real good. In fact, after the incident with Shirley at the hospital, she looked better than ever.

"Oh, Paul, I am so glad to see you. They made me stay in jail for two nights until your lawyer and Marlene convinced them I wasn't a murderer. Or at least, convinced them that I wasn't leaving town."

I didn't tell her that the real reason was that my mouthpiece put up bail in the amount of $5000, the interest going on my bill. We said goodbye to Vose and headed out. I told Betty that we had a meeting with "DC" McGuire, parking expert, in a couple of hours. We could drive out to the Rancho Park golf course, have lunch, and see him when he finished his round.

"DC" came off the 18th green and made a beeline for the bar where we waited. I introduced "DC" and Betty, and "DC" immediately started talking about her notebook.

I took out my copy and Betty was peppered with questions. It was just as "DC" had thought. The numbers were tickets with entry and exit times. The notations showed how much should have been deposited, and how much really was. He confirmed it. Although the garage collected an average of $250 each day, the day manager deposited between $700 and $1000 each working day. The laundry was in full swing.

I told "DC" that it made no sense. The mob was trying to buy Art Bell's operation. Why would it launder money though a garage that it didn't own?

"I never said the money came from the mob," he said. At that moment the confusion that had haunted me since the beginning of this case began to lift.

"DC" complimented Betty on her notebook and told her that she was doing a terrific job as garage manager. She blushed and said that as night manager, she had a lot of time on her hands. "DC" was mumbling something about wanting to get back into the parking business and looking for the right person to handle the operations when the bartender, who was holding a phone, asked if there was a Paul Manning in the room.

I walked over to the bar, said, "Guilty as charged," and he handed me the instrument.

I answered, "Manning."

The voice at the other end was very familiar. It was reminiscent of Roman moonlight but now it had an edge, much like that she-wolf in Sicily. "You were warned, Mr. Manning. I guess you didn't understand. Therefore we will have to show you how we operate. If you remember, I gave you three names of people whose health would be in jeopardy if you didn't stop intruding into our affairs. I have one of those people here as my guest. I now must figure out what to do with her. By the way, I saw you at the bar of the Bel Air hotel. I assume you now know my identity. That makes the problem even more difficult." The line went dead.

Let's see, she named three people, Betty, Shirley and me. Well, I was looking at Betty. Oh my God! They had Shirley. Suddenly our little tiff at the hospital seemed inconsequential. Nurse Mary and beautiful Betty disappeared from my mind. I ran out of the bar and jumped into my car. It was only when I put my key in the ignition that I realized I had absolutely no idea what to do next.

9

Bel Air Patrol to the Rescue

I sat there in the parking lot, watching golfers on the practice green. Where was Shirley? Even if I knew, what could I do?

I knew they were probably holding her in the mansion where I was taken when I had been kidnapped. That was in Bel Air. Maybe a conversation with Bel Air Patrol head Capt. Hankins and my buddy Jim Walsh might shed some light on the case. It was at least a place to start.

The patrol had its offices in East Gate, one of the two gated entrances to the star-studded Bel-Air section of L.A. The headquarters looked like a Spanish-tiled private home, except for the patrol cars parked outside. Most people didn't know it, but you could see many more Hollywood types by standing at East Gate around 7:30 AM when they left for the studio than at the clubs in the evenings. Of course, catching a glimpse wasn't easy, because one of the patrol's main jobs was to protect the privacy of the residents.

We also provided other services. In addition to picking up the afore-mentioned kidnapped son, we would drive past one particular house at the same time every night. If the front light was on, we would go in and lift a very famous, very overweight director into bed. No one ever said a word, not us, not the director (he was out), not his wife. There was always hot coffee and cookies for us when we left.

In another case, a very famous rock star's son was smoking something he shouldn't, fell asleep, and started a fire. The patrol got the alarm, arrived well ahead of the fire department, and found the door locked. We broke a small pane of glass, opened the door, carried the young man to safety and put out the fire. The next week we got a bill from the famous rock star for the broken window.

Hankins had hired me after the LAPD gave me the ax and taken me under his wing. I was part of patrol, but I also worked with the Captain when he was asked by some of the residents of Bel Air to help when they didn't want the police involved. I left to become a PI, but maintained a relationship with the Captain and my friends on the patrol.

"So, Manning, I understand you've been busy since we picked you up after your kidnapping," Hankins said as I strolled in. "How's the head?" He had contacts everywhere and knew everything that went on in LA's law enforcement.

"Oh, I'm fine. But I need your help. Shirley has been kidnapped by the bunch that picked me up and is being threatened. Any ideas?"

"Well," Hankins said, "we know the general area where we lost them when we followed you after you had been kidnapped. I have a list of every house in the area, and perhaps by the process of elimination, we can figure out where she's being held."

The Captain and I reviewed the list. It was like Hollywood's A-list. Surely no one in this group could be part of the deal. Then I noticed that one of the names on the list wasn't a person but a company: Silver Screen Corp.

I asked about it, and the Captain told me that a number of the homes in Bel Air were listed by the names of holding companies to protect the privacy of the owners. I asked if he knew who owned Silver Screen.

"Sure, RKO Pictures."

It clicked. When I recognized my kidnapper at the Bel Air Hotel, Shirley had told me that she was an ex-girlfriend of Howard Hughes. And Hughes owned RKO. I put two and two together and started to run out the door.

"Where you going?" The Captain's tone stopped me cold.

"After Shirley," I said.

Hankins explained as only he can that waltzing into a nest of mobsters alone and without a plan was probably a ticket to Forest Lawn, the cemetery to the stars. He said the resources of the patrol were at my service and he had a plan.

Seems the Silver Screen house was covered by the patrol's alarm system. He would give me a uniform, and five of the patrol's finest would "respond" to a silent alarm at the house. That would at least get us inside and give us an excuse to look the place over. We could play it by ear from there.

With my pal Jim Walsh driving and the other three following in a second car, we roared into the driveway and raced to the front door. Not waiting to knock, we tumbled in and started to search the house, guns drawn.

Three gunsels met us coming down the main staircase. Since we had our guns out and ready and they didn't, we had them in handcuffs before they could say much at all.

Walsh and I looked through the downstairs and found Shirley, blindfolded and tied up, in a small room under the stairs. We grabbed her and were headed for the stairs when a voice I would recognize anywhere—one now with the growl of a she wolf—stopped us in our tracks.

She was standing on the steps, dressed as if she were about to receive an Academy Award. I could tell from her tone and the look on her face that she wasn't happy.

"Round two goes to you, Mr. Manning. I wouldn't, however, become too confident. I know what I want and I know how to get it. You have been warned for the last time."

Walsh and I grabbed Shirley and the six of us left quickly, jumped in our cars and returned to the Bel Air Patrol office. Shirley had forgotten about the "incident" at the hospital and was very glad to see me. I had Walsh take her home and stay with her. I had another person I wanted to see.

Art Ball owned the parking company the Mob was trying to take over. He also was laundering money through his parking garages. His mansion was only about half a mile away, so it was a short drive. I had some very specific questions for Betty's employer.

It was a replay of the last time I had been at Ball's house. The front door was open. The houseman, Jeeves, was standing in the entryway. He had a dazed look on his face.

Behind him, sprawled in the doorway to the library, was a body. It had a bullet hole in the forehead. I knew only one thing for sure: Art Ball would be Forest Lawn's next customer.

10

The Mystery Unravels, Sort of

I took Jeeves into the library and poured him a dram of Laphroaig. He downed it in a single gulp. Fortified, he told me the story.

Turns out that Jeeves was more than just Ball's houseman. He was also his personal assistant. He knew everything.

"I've been with Art for almost 10 years. In the beginning, it was just a parking operation and we grew quickly. But Art became greedy. Parking wasn't enough for him. He began to dabble in numbers, prostitution, gambling. When he found out how easy it was to launder money through the garage, it was icing on the cake.

"I had no problem with the numbers, gambling and all," Jeeves said. "I was making a lot of money. But it began to go south when the Mob arrived. They didn't want the garage; they wanted Art's entire operation. The idiot, he should have let them have it. He had all the money he needed. But Art decided to fight them. And that woman, what a piece of work."

"Woman?" I asked. "Do you mean Maria LaFlonza?"

"Yeah, that's her. She was a 'B' actress, but used that as a cover. She runs the Mob operation here on the West Coast. And she wants Art's setup in the worst way. I guess she'll get it now."

I heard a sound in the next room, and one of LaFlonza's gunsels walked in with his gun trained on us. At that moment, a car pulled up outside. The lady herself swept in with two more of her pack. It just kept getting better and better.

"Well, Mr. Manning," LaFlonza snarled, "it looks like this round is going to be mine."

She looked over at her man.

"Sorry, boss," he said. "I had to shoot Ball. He was going for his gun."

"That's all right," she said. "Actually, it makes matters easier. We'll just shoot Manning with Ball's gun, put your gun in Manning's hands, and we'll come out clean."

I didn't like the way this was going, at all.

"Wait just a minute," I said. "You can't go around shooting people. I assume you killed Gilberto Quintana at the garage and set up my client to take the fall?"

"Ah, Gilberto," she purred. "He was a nice guy, and a great lover. But he just couldn't get it right. I thought I had control of him, but it turned out he was spying for Ball, not for me. I met him at the garage that night. We were going to a late dinner. When I mentioned his double-dealing, he was understandably upset. I'm afraid the knife is my weapon of choice.

"As for your client, she just happened to be conveniently nearby.

"OK, fellas, let's do this," LaFlonza said. "Someone may have heard the shots. Jeeves, give the guys a hand with Ball's body."

I looked at Jeeves, and he smiled. "Well," he shrugged, "she pays top dollar."

This wasn't looking good. I was running out of options, and I didn't hear the cavalry coming over the hill. No one had called the police. Jeeves and another of the mobsters moved Ball's body so it looked as if he was shooting at something. Then they shoved me over in front of the body. Jeeves took Ball's gun and pointed it at my chest. No, this wasn't looking good at all.

At that moment, a thick Irish brogue cut through the tension. “Hold it right there, boyo, and drop that gun.”

My buddy Jim Walsh from the Bel Air Patrol entered the room. “Thought you could use a little help about now, Paul.”

I started to breathe again.

Seems Jim had asked one of his Patrol buddies to take Shirley home and then followed me over to Ball’s house. He got there just in time to see LaFlonza arrive, and had been standing behind the door with his gun drawn during the entire affair.

I picked up the phone and called Bill Vose. He said he would dispatch a car and be right over. When he arrived, Bill flashed his badge for all to see, and I told the story. He arrested LaFlonza and her bunch on the spot.

“You’re wasting your time, officer,” she said. “My lawyers will have us out of jail before lunch.”

“Perhaps,” Vose said. “But with the testimony of Manning and Walsh, plus the fact that the knife in your purse is a perfect match to the one we found in Quintana, my guess is that the jury won’t have much trouble coming to a decision. Take her away.”

“I think this round is mine,” I said as LaFlonza walked out in handcuffs, “Game Set Match.”

The next day, Shirley and I met with DC McGuire, our parking expert; my client, Betty Beeson; and Betty’s landlady, Marlene Crowley, for lunch at the 19th hole at Rancho Park Golf Course.

“What I don’t understand,” said Crowley, “is why the Mob cared so much about the notebook that had the money-laundering information. They nearly killed Betty and ripped her room apart looking for it.”

"They didn't," I said. "That was one of Ball's guys. Ball would have been in big trouble with the feds if Betty had figured out what was going on and turned him in. Ball was just fortunate that she was from Iowa and not Manhattan. She didn't know what she had in the notebook. The Mob was interested in Ball's other activities. The money laundering was just an 'extra' for them."

"So, Betty, what's next for you?" I asked. "Your former boss is pushing up daisies."

"Betty and I have decided to enter into a partnership," DC said. "I will front for her, and she can run the operations. Parking operations, that is. Our first location will be the Argyle, arranged through the contacts Shirley can provide."

It all seemed to have worked out. The murderer was in jail, Betty and DC were in business, and then I looked at Shirley.

"I think it's time you made a choice, Paul Manning," she said. "Me or that endless line of nurses and waitresses and beautiful clients."

Shirley gave me a look that told me I had little choice. I began to wonder if I would have been better off back with the Sicilian she-wolf.

At that moment, the bartender called my name and said I had a phone call. It was my answering service. Seems a new client had called, and it was an emergency. I asked whether the client was female. The answer was yes. I was in trouble again.

But there's more to this story. One unanswered question:

"Why did Betty lie about how Quintana died? Remember the famous life-saving rubber plant?"

Look for the solution to this riddle in a future episode of Death by Parking.

Episode Two

The Phantom

1

Basis in Fact

"Dad, I can't sleep."

Huh? I checked the clock; it was 4:15 in the morning. What was Paulo doing standing next to my bed? Particularly since he was 16 years old. Shirley was in Kansas, visiting her folks, and we were batching it. Sixteen-year-olds simply don't come into the bedroom and profess to fright. Something was going on.

"What's the problem?"

"I can't sleep. I keep thinking about what I heard at school today. It's about a haunted parking garage. I know it can't be true, but since most rumors have some basis in fact, it's keeping me awake."

"Basis in fact." It's three hours before breakfast and my son is talking about "basis in fact"?

I'm Paul Manning, and I'm a private investigator. I got my start nearly 20 years ago by solving a murder that took place in a parking garage in Hollywood. I also married Paulo's (that's my son, Paul Manning Jr.) mother and expanded my agency. We were pretty successful, able to move out of my "film noir" office on Hollywood Boulevard to a nice single-story on Sunset Strip. We hired a few operatives and, with Shirley running the office, built a successful and lucrative business.

Paulo is a bright kid. He's doing well in school, has a lot of friends, and I'm hoping he will follow me in the business. But "basis in fact" at 4 a.m.? I needed to get to the bottom of this.

"OK, OK, but I need some coffee."

"I already put it on." The kid was resourceful, too.

We lived in a large "California Bungalow" off Mulholland Drive above the Strip. When Shirley and I married, I had a small place up the road, but I knew a family was coming and we would need a larger place. This one was perfect. We had an incredible view of the LA Basin. On clear mornings, you could see from the Hollywood sign and downtown, past Century City and Santa Monica to the Pacific. In the evenings, Paulo and I would sit on the deck and watch the planes line up to land at LAX. Once he counted more than 30 planes in the final approach pattern to the country's third-busiest airport.

As I looked out over the city at 4 a.m., I was greeted by a wall of darkness. Not a city light to be seen. Power failure? Nope. "June Gloom." The marine layer was in, and it was thick. Our house was surrounded by clouds, and the basin was covered with a layer that would, I hoped, burn off by noon. In the meantime, famous LA with its palm trees and pretty girls in shorts and tank-tops was cold, wet and gloomy. The perfect setting for a chat about "basis in fact."

Paulo brought my coffee and began his story.

"It's that idiot Billy Bronson. He is always talking about something that you can't believe. The other day he claimed to have seen a UFO. It was obvious to everyone that it was a police chopper running down a gang-banger. You can see those spotlights miles away. But this time was different."

I went into detective mode. Good PI's listen more than they talk. It's hard to get to the bottom of something with your mouth open. I knew that Paulo would get to the point soon. And he did.

"Yesterday, Billy was jabbering on about something or other when he got really quiet. He took me into the boy's bathroom and checked to be sure the place was empty—you know, like the mob guys do in the movies, looking under the stall doors and all.

"He told me that the old parking garage on Olympic just east of the campus was haunted. He said he heard sounds and saw lights flashing there late at night. Dad, he was really scared.

"I asked him when this had happened, and Billy said he'd seen the lights and heard the sounds a couple of times when he had walked home late after music practice. And night before last, a 'ghost' had come out and told him to 'get lost.' He ran all the way home.

"I know Billy pretty well, Dad, and I can tell when he's telling the truth. This was the truth. I've been thinking about it and maybe something is going on in that garage. I think we should investigate."

There were a couple of words he used that began to worry me—"we" and "investigate." But I knew Paulo was stubborn and maybe this would be a good lesson for him, teach him something about my world. Sure, why not. We could go down to the structure, stake it out, have some great father-son time, and he would see that the whole thing was just a figment of a teenager's imagination.

"So what do you propose we do?" I asked.

"Well, we could call Uncle Bill and he could stake out the place and catch the bad guys in the act."

"Uncle Bill" was Bill Vose, my closest friend, Paulo's uncle by friendship, and a captain in the LAPD. I could just see me making that call. Bill would still be laughing half an hour after he hung up on me.

"Before we get that far, maybe we should check it out ourselves. That way we can give more information to Bill and he can be better prepared." (And when it turned out to be nothing, we wouldn't embarrass ourselves.)

"So you think we should stake it out ourselves?"

"Great idea. What time does Billy's music class end?"

The deal was struck, and at 10 p.m., father and son were sitting in my Subaru Outback across the street from a relatively disreputable-looking parking structure.

The place had to have been built 30 years ago. It was small, dark, and from what I could tell, closed for the day. It looked like it provided parking for a couple of the1960s-style office buildings located in the area around Olympic and Bundy. The owner had planted bushes and shrubs to try to spruce up the place, but it hadn't worked.

This was a neighborhood in the process of change. My guess was that the garage wasn't long for this world. Buildings were going up everywhere nearby. It was becoming a "media" district with MTV, ESPN, Fox News, and Skywalker Sound offices all within a couple of blocks. There were at least four buildings of substantial size going up. Construction cranes were on every corner. But at 10 p.m., it was quiet.

The garage in question was three stories. There was one entrance and exit with the requisite white booth and gates. I had learned about the parking business during our first adventure and knew that a lot of money probably passed through that booth every day. How much actually got into the owner's bank account was another story.

It was 10:15, and Paulo was beginning to fidget. I had brought some cocoa. Stakeouts were nothing if not boring. Teenage boys bore quickly. I was about to suggest that we call it a night when Paulo pointed to the garage. There was a glow coming from the rear of the second-floor. We got out of the car and walked toward the garage.

As we reached the sidewalk in front of the entrance, we heard something that sounded to me like machinery. There was no grind of motors but a clanking like chains being dropped on the floor. Like someone in leg irons was moving slowly across the second deck.

Then Paulo grabbed my arm and pointed up. There was, I kid you not, an apparition walking along, I guess you could call it, a "parapet." It was bent over and seemed to be dragging a foot. It reminded me of someone you would name "Igor." Paulo dove behind one bush, I took another.

As Sherlock Holmes would have said: "The game's afoot."

2

He Had No Fear

There I was, lying on my belly at 10:30 p.m., hiding from a ghost. Oh, come on. this was ridiculous. I looked over at Paulo, who was obviously thinking the same thing. He was now on his knees and trying to get a better look at the "thing" moving about the second floor. I was proud of my boy; he had no fear.

It was hard to see what was going on. Of course, it was night, and the garage lights were off. An engine seemed to be running in the back, and what light there was flickered, then seemed to get stronger as the engine sounds increased.

We decided to go back to the car and regroup.

"Come on, Dad, let's go over and check it out."

That Paulo, he was always ready to head straight into the fray. Time to teach him a little finesse.

"OK, OK. We can do that. But it might be better if we can figure out what's going on. Tell you what. Let's go around to the side where we passed that stairwell and try to get a better idea of what we're dealing with before we simply walk in and make complete fools of ourselves."

I could tell Paulo wasn't buying it, but he said nothing. We quietly walked around to the side of the building, found the open stairwell, and crept up to the second deck. Paulo was kneeling in front of me as I slowly opened the door.

Naturally, it hadn't been oiled in years and sounded like we were entering the dungeon in Dracula's castle. This just couldn't get any weirder.

Paulo stuck his head around the door and said, "Dad, they are loading some stuff into the back of a truck and leaving. Let's go get 'em."

"Get 'em"—he had been watching too much television.

We weren't armed. Who knew what they had. Plus, I had a 16-year-old boy with me. I pulled him back into the stairwell and listened as the truck drove out of the lot. We ran to the edge of the deck and watched it move at an unconcerned pace down the street.

"Damn," I said. "Looks like we missed them."

"Well, maybe so," said Paulo, "but I got their license number. Now maybe Uncle Bill and the LAPD can help."

What a kid. He has my genes. As we left the garage, we found the name of the owner on the side of the booth, S and J Investments. The office was in the Olympic and Bundy towers just around the corner.

I let him call Bill Vose; figured he wouldn't hang up quite so quickly on his "nephew." Sure enough, Paulo came into my office the next afternoon with a big smile on his face.

"Uncle Bill said I should tell you that I don't have a PI license and shouldn't be sneaking around garages in the middle of the night. Then he gave me the registered owner of the truck, and told me to tell you that you owed him a bottle of 20-year-old Glenfiddich."

Wow, running that license plate was expensive—that's over 70 bucks.

Yes, I admit it, I'm a whisky fan. That's Scotch whisky to you. And, in my case, single malt. I love the rich peaty taste of an Islay malt. I had been working Bill for years to wean him off that sweet bourbon swill he drank. Glenfiddich is a mild, single-malt, and a good choice for the novice. But a bottle of

20-year-old? "So," I asked Paulo, "where would you say we go from here?"

"The truck is registered to a rental company near the airport. We could go ask who rented it and then ask them what the heck they were doing at the garage."

OK, it was time to introduce Paulo to the economics of the PI business. We had no client. No one was paying us to do this, and I doubted that Billy, his school friend, was going to pony up $75-an-hour plus expenses to find out that his "ghost" was a couple of guys in a truck. I explained this to Paulo.

"Dad, why don't we go to the owner and tell him someone was messing around in his garage? He would hire us to find out who was doing what and solve the case."

OK, not bad thinking. The kid had a head for the business.

The next afternoon, we were sitting in front of Ray Schumer, the "S" of "S and J Investments." I told him I was a PI and my son had noticed something at his garage around the corner. We thought we should discuss it with him.

He was a great guy and smiled at Paulo. "OK, son, tell me the story."

When Paulo finished, Schumer began to laugh. He was almost in tears before he got hold of himself. He rummaged through his desk and came up with a business card, then handed to me.

"Deswal Consulting—Garage Restorations."

Huh? What did a consulting firm have to do with sounds and lights in a parking garage late at night? Schumer thought it was funny; I was confused, and just a little pissed off. He was laughing at my son, and no one, I mean, no one laughs at my son.

I was just about to give Schumer a piece of my mind when his assistant walked into the office and said: “Sorry to interrupt, Ray, but we have a problem.

“They found a body in the shrubbery next to the garage on Le Grand. It was one of the crew from the restoration firm. He was shot.”

“Well, Manning, I may need your services after all.”

3

No Ghosts

Timing is everything. I was about to blow up at Schumer when we learned there was a serious problem at his garage: a dead body. OK, fair enough. But what the hell did the apparition my son and I had seen with our own eyes at the garage have to do with a parking consulting firm?

I was able to regain my composure and said, "Well, then, Mr. Schumer, perhaps you might fill us in." I glanced over at Paulo and could see that my use of "us" had hit its mark. He was beaming.

"Here's the deal," Schumer started. "Buildings are made up of concrete and steel. First, the rebar is set in place and the concrete is poured around it. When that dries, you have a rock-solid structure that should stand for a lifetime, if not a lot longer.

"Parking garages age faster than your usual concrete structure," he said. "In a traditional building, the outer walls seal off the insides from the weather, from severe temperature changes. And frankly, people don't usually bring in items from the outside that would affect the structural integrity of such a building.

"A garage is different. It's wide open. Rain, wind, cold, and heat impact the concrete floors. See, the water gets into tiny cracks, and over the years expansion and contraction allow water into the rebar. Then it rusts, and as it does, it expands and breaks off chunks of the concrete. If this goes on too long, the entire structure could be at risk. The trouble is you can't tell when the rebar is starting to rust. It happens inside the concrete.

"Now, there are some pretty high-tech—and expensive—ways to stop the rusting," Schumer said. "You can spend a fortune and put an electrical charge on the steel. But that might or might not work. The best thing to do is to take care of your garage. Keep it clean, sweep out any salt that might get tracked in, and be sure no water can freeze inside the structure.

"We just bought that garage on Le Grand and, frankly, its previous owners weren't too careful about maintenance. So we brought in a firm to find out whether we needed to make any repairs or, if the problem was bad enough, to replace the garage. That's what you and your boy saw last night," he said. "They were testing the floors, and they can do it only at night when the garage is empty. They drag chains across the floor and can tell by the sound whether the rebar is rusting. It's something of an art and requires experience. Deswal Consulting is one of the best," Schumer said.

"But why would anyone want to kill an employee of a firm testing a garage?" I asked. "Is there a lot riding on the results?"

"It doesn't make much sense to me, either," he said. "The result of the testing was going to be expensive for us, either way. We would either spend millions repairing this garage or spend millions building a new one. In the general scheme of things, it didn't make a lot of difference.

"However, they were working for me," Schumer said. "Can you do what you do and find out what's going on? We need to put this thing to bed as quickly as possible."

"Mr. Schumer, we would be happy to investigate. But understand that the police will be all over this. We will be working around the periphery; they will control the case."

"Come on, Manning, I know how you PIs work," Schumer said. "You have contacts everywhere. In fact, I wouldn't be surprised if that fellow at the police department is one of your best friends. Keep me posted."

I told him we would send a contract and we left. Paulo and I walked around the corner and, sure enough, enough police units had arrived at the parking garage to give the impression of a patrolmen's convention, or a donut shop.

Schumer was prescient. The lead detective was Bill Vose, my old partner at the LAPD. He smiled and gave Paulo a hug.

"When am I getting my whisky?" he asked me. Bill had run a truck license plate for Paulo and claimed that was worth a $70 bottle of Glenfiddich.

"Give me a break, Bill. I found out I owed you only yesterday," I said, glaring at Paulo, who was still smiling ear to ear. Bill laughed and began to fill us in.

"We got the call about an hour and a half ago," he said. "A gardener found the body behind some bushes, at the front of the garage. It looks as if he was shot and then pushed off an upper floor of the garage. We found blood up on the fourth floor, almost straight up from here. Coroner says the poor fellow has been dead for at least a day and a half. That would place the murder on the night before last."

I looked at Paulo and his face said, "This is up to you, Dad, I'm over my head," so I decided to set an example. "Paulo and I were here at the garage night before last checking out some strange noises. We saw a garage construction crew at work but nothing else."

"I might have known you would be involved," Bill said. "No blonde in this one, Paul. Are you keeping it G-rated because of Paulo here?"

Bill's reference to the fact that many of my clients had been female and the majority blonde sent Paulo into spasms of teenage laughter. I just smiled and told Bill that we had been hired by the owners to look into it. Bill said he would be happy to have us on board. I was sure that was true—at least until he got his whisky.

We left Bill, climbed back in our car, and sat for a few minutes to discuss our next move. "What do we do now?" I asked Paulo.

"Well, we could just leave the forensic stuff to Uncle Bill; I'm sure he'll fill us in later. And we could start our investigation by talking to the consulting company, this fellow's co-workers."

The kid was right on the money. He was going to be an asset to the firm when he was old enough to get his PI's license.

As I drove through the garage and entered the second floor, a white van—with the word "Deswal" and a stylized logo painted on the side— going about 5 miles an hour smashed into the side of our car.

That would have been bad enough, but when I looked over at the driver's side of the van, I found the spot behind the wheel empty. First, ghosts dragging chains across the floor, then a phantom driver. This was getting to be too much.

4

A Possible Reason

Paulo grabbed the door handle and tried to open the door. It was either jammed or held shut by the van. I jumped out and he followed on my side. When I got to the driver's side, I had to make a split-second decision: Was it time for Paulo to see his first dead body? It was decided for me.

"Oh, gross," was all my teenager said, as he peered over my shoulder.

The driver had been shot in the chest and, judging by the amount of blood, not too long ago. I told Paulo to run down and get Bill, who was supervising the LAPD crime scene team in the brush where the first body was found. He arrived with an escort in white coats about three minutes later.

"Cripes, Manning. Don't we have enough on our plate?"

A quick look told me we should step out of the way and let Bill and his team do their job. It was just as well. If we were going to get any information in this now series of murders, we needed to get to Deswal Consulting, and we needed to get there before the police did.

"No problem, Bill. By the way, do you have an ID on this fellow?"

"He's an engineer with Deswal. His name is Frank Straer. The other one's name is Charles Segal. I think Straer was the boss. The title 'senior' was on his card."

I saw Paulo taking notes, so I didn't. We left the car there. Bill would let me know when they untangled everything and we could retrieve the Outback. From past experience, I knew there was a rental joint a few blocks away. Seems I'm always bending cars the wrong way. We walked over and had a new set of wheels in a few minutes. Next stop, Deswal Consulting.

Their local offices were located in Burbank, in an office building near the airport. We decided not to take the freeway, but went down Olympic to Highland, and then over to Cahuenga, around the back lot of Universal Studios and into the heart of studio-land.

Most people think Hollywood is where you'll find the studios. Except for Paramount and a couple of smaller specialty lots, they are either in Culver City (Sony) or Burbank, where within half a mile you'll find Disney, Universal, Warner Bros., plus the TV studios ABC, NBC and CBS.

Disney is investing millions in the area, so high-rises are springing up and being leased by film support teams and production companies. The city was made famous by "Tonight Show" host Johnny Carson and his line about the show coming from "Beautiful Downtown Burbank." It may not be a garden spot, but it has changed since Carson moved his desk from Manhattan.

If my life is a movie, this was certainly the place to make it.

We arrived across from the entrance to the airport and parked. I knew the fellow who owned the complex, which included an eight-story office building, a Hilton and a small convention center. The proximity to the airport was good for business. He was able to offer parking for people who were flying out. He used the hotel vans to transport folks back and forth.

He told me his biggest problem with the parking was theft. One day, he was returning from a trip and the van driver tried to sell him a parking ticket issued that day. Seems the idea was that if he threw away his ticket and used the one proffered by the driver, he would save considerably on his parking fee.

Boy, did that driver get the wrong customer. I guess the van drivers would take a ticket to get in the lot (instead of using their access cards), and then sell the "new" ticket to folks who had parked there for a week or more. The drivers would make a few bucks, the parkers would save a few bucks, and my friend would be out a few bucks.

The Deswal branch manager, Frank Straer, was not there, which we knew, but his second-in-command, Martina Smithson, could see us. I looked at Paulo and he just shook his head. The kid knew the next conversation wasn't going to be pretty.

We sat in Smithson's office and I broke the sad news. I have found that the best approach is to just tell the facts, quickly and without a lot of detail. It hurts just as much, but it's over quicker.

Smithson was tough. She was about my age and obviously experienced. She was upset but pulled herself together quickly and asked how we were involved. I explained. She looked at Paulo with a suspicious eye but said nothing.

I asked her what she knew about the project, and she began to fill us in.

"Well, Frank was supervising the testing. My background is more centered on operations. We had been on the job about a week, working from one floor to the next. My understanding was that the job was going well. Frank thought that the garage could be saved, and only certain areas would need repair. The garage was built in 1962, but with Southern California being a temperate climate, there wasn't much salt and ice to create 'spalling' in the garage. "

Smithson began to explain about spalling and concrete pulling away from rusting rebar, but I told her we had already been given an overview, and wanted to focus on why there were two dead bodies on this job.

"I have no idea," Smithson said. "All I know is that this morning, Frank got a call and ran out of the office. I asked him what was up, and all he said was, 'It's better you don't know until we get this all straightened out.'"

I left my card with her, and Paulo and I headed back to the office.

"You know, Dad, I've been thinking. What would they do in this garage that could upset someone so much they would kill over it? Maybe there's a body buried in one of the floors and they are afraid the repair guys will find it. Someone that disappeared in 1962 when the concrete was wet."

I pulled over to the side of the road and put the car in park. Paulo gave me that innocent 16-year-old look of, "what?"

"You may be on to something, Paulo. But killing the contractor wouldn't put a stop to the job. My guess is that something has already been found and Messrs. Segal and Straer found it. And they may have been trying to sell it. We had better look into who else is involved in this project. They're probably in danger, too."

5

We Get a Hint

Our next step was to get more information about that garage and its construction. We called the owner but he wasn't much help. Ray Schumer, the new owner, knew little of the origins of the place. He recommended that we contact a Westside developer who worked there nearly 40 years ago.

Rick Johnson was retired. He lived in a beautiful home in Westwood, near UCLA. Its red-brick facade was partly covered with vines. The 100-foot walk was lined by impatiens. The place had to be 7,500 square feet and who knew what size pool was in the back. I guess property development paid well.

Shirley (thank heaven she was back from visiting her folks) had called ahead and we were expected. Johnson opened the door and directed us to a den-like room off the front hallway.

"Shouldn't you be in school?" he asked Paulo.

"It's spring break and I'm giving my dad a hand," he responded. I was pleased that he didn't sound like a smartass, just a teenager explaining what was what. This seemed to placate Johnson.

I told him what had brought us there and that we were looking for information pertaining to that parking structure 30 years ago. Johnson sat behind his desk, reached down to a drawer, and pulled out a bottle. It was 20-year-old Glenlivet. He offered me a "splash," and who am I to turn down a drink? I wanted to make Johnson feel comfortable, right? He told Paulo to go over to the wet bar and help himself to a soda. He said he liked to keep the single-malt close at hand. I understood perfectly.

"The construction boom hadn't really begun yet on the west side in the early '60s," Johnson said. "We built the garage you mentioned to support a number of low-rise projects in the area, most of which have been torn down to make way for all those mid-rise buildings on Olympic and Centinela. I understand that Schumer was trying to decide whether to tear down the garage or replace it. Makes sense; those things have a shelf life of only 30 to 40 years anyway."

I explained about the murders and Paulo's idea that something might be encased in the garage's concrete floor.

Johnson gave Paulo an appraising look and then his friendly attitude changed almost immediately. "That's the most ridiculous thing I have ever heard. Who would be shoving something in wet concrete? There would be too many people around. When we do a pour, we pour an entire floor at a time. They don't stop. There would be no opportunity for someone to put something in the wet 'mud.' You two have wasted enough of my time."

And with that, he stood up. We got the idea and left.

"I think we have a suspect," Paulo said when we got back in the car. "He reacted too strongly. He knows something he's not telling us."

I was about to pull away when a woman came out from around the side of the house and approached the car. She was about Johnson's age and beautiful. I started to introduce myself when she held up her hand.

"I was never here and you didn't hear this from me. They were pouring the floors on that garage in early August of 1962. A lot was going on then, and some very important people wanted things hushed up. If certain people knew that the garage was being torn down or opened up, it could change what we know about much of the history of the '60s." With that said, she walked away.

Paulo gave me a questioning look. We needed to talk to that woman again.

This brought back memories of my parking caper in the late '50s. It involved the mob, Howard Hughes, the FBI, the CIA, and the Kennedys. Those guys with funny noses from New Jersey and Las Vegas were moving into Los Angeles. The LAPD had them under control, but a lot of crazy things happened during those so-called "Camelot years." The Vietnam War, free love, drugs everywhere, and a new very popular president who could do no wrong. But what happened in L.A. in August 1962?

The only thing I could remember was the death of Marilyn Monroe.

6

Our Lives Become Complicated

So what else happened in August of 1962? We went to the L.A. Times and gained access to its morgue. That's what newspapers call their library. We checked the paper thoroughly. There was nothing, nada, zip, except the tragic death of the movie goddess.

Marilyn Monroe had been found by her housekeeper in her Brentwood home. The L.A. County coroner's report showed no foul play. It reported she had overdosed on sedatives prescribed to her. Her death was ruled a "probable suicide." But rumors swirled.

She partied with the "Rat Pack," and in those days, one of its stalwart members was Peter Lawford, President Kennedy's brother-in-law. Monroe supposedly had an affair with JFK.

Of course, the conspiracy nuts came out of the woodwork. Everyone from the FBI and CIA to aliens from outer space were supposed to have been involved in her death. As with most conspiracy theories, these were strongly denied and discounted by all involved.

But what if...

Good detectives don't speculate. They get facts, look for data, run timelines, and poke holes in other people's stories. Speculating on a death nearly 45 years old, even one of a movie star, was fruitless. We needed more information; we needed to talk to that woman at Rick Johnson's home.

Paulo and I were pretty sure she was his wife. She was the right age, and she was present at his house. A bit of research in the morgue and we found that her name was Helen, and a picture in the society pages of The Times confirmed our theory. The problem was how were we going to get her to talk to us, and keep her husband out of it, at least for now?

We looked back through the society pages and found that she was a member of the Riviera Tennis Club on Motor Avenue. Although the place was a bit ritzy for my blood, I had a friend who moved in those circles. He was CEO of a small finance company but had made a good living. I called him and he told me that a Clarence Jackson sat on the board and would help.

My friend paved the way, and I called Jackson, who was able to obtain Helen Johnson's tennis schedule. She was slated for a lesson that afternoon.

Paulo and I dropped by the house to don some "tennis" clothes and headed down Laurel Canyon to Sunset, across to La Cienega and then to over Pico. Motor ends at Pico, with the Fox Studios. The area is upscale. A perfect place for a tennis club.

We turned left on Motor, drove through the Rancho Park Golf Course, and were giving the car to the valet at the Riviera just as Mrs. Johnson was starting her lesson.

We sat in the bleachers and watched a bronze-god-tennis pro put her through her paces. In 30 minutes or so, she had finished and started back toward the clubhouse. Paulo walked up and asked her to join us. How could she turn down a cute 16-year-old in tennis togs? She looked puzzled at first, then when she recognized me, very concerned.

"Mrs. Johnson," I said, "I'm Paul Manning, and this is my son, Paul. We need to follow-up on our conversation this morning. You mentioned 'certain people' and 'changing history.' We need more to go on than that."

She appeared nervous and looked about with furtive glances as if this were a clandestine meeting in a back alley, not the bleachers of the Riviera Tennis Club.

"I can't talk to you. There's just too much going on." She started to stand up and I caught her arm.

"Look, Mrs. Johnson, we just need a hint. The only thing we found that of interest in August of 1962 was the death of Marilyn Monroe."

Mrs. Johnson looked confused, then surprised, and then started to laugh. "No, they didn't bury Marilyn in the garage, if that's what you mean. This has nothing to do with her. I would suggest you spend less time at the newspaper library and more time at the County Recorder's Office." With that she got up and strode off.

"County Recorder's Office?" said Paulo. "What do they record?"

"Let's go back to the car. I'll explain on the way."

I told Paulo that the Recorder's Office is where all the records are kept as to who owns what in real estate within the county. It also keeps records of marriages and divorces and all major business and financial transactions. In some cases, I told him, you can trace land ownership all the way back to the Land Grants given to court favorites by the king of Spain.

The king granted large tracts of land to his friends and allies, and when the U.S. took over California, it agreed by treaty that it would honor those grants. However, nothing is quite that simple. Congress changed the rules after the Gold Rush, and many grants were contested in court.

It was a real mess, I told Paulo, and just who owned what began to blur. Often the cost of litigation was more than the land was worth.

I was proud to have remembered what Miss Weaver taught in my seventh-grade California History class. Paulo was impressed.

When we arrived at the Recorder's Office in Norwalk, a small city southeast of downtown Los Angeles, we asked to see the history of the land where the garage was built.

It took a few minutes for the clerk to find the microfilm and queue it up for us. There it was, plain as day, Johnson's company had purchased the land from Caldwell Properties. But it all seemed completely above-board.

"Who is Caldwell?" Paulo asked.

We searched the Recorder's databases, and after a number of false leads, we found the owner of Caldwell Properties. It was a New Jersey-based partnership: "Palermo Ltd."

We could have dug deeper, but I didn't think it was necessary. Our lives had become much more complicated.

Helen Johnson's husband had purchased the land where the garage stood—and where two people had been killed—from the mob.

7

PAULO A TARGET? OVER MY...

I had a problem. First of all, I didn't like dealing with the fellows with bent noses and names that end in vowels. My last experience, also involving a parking operation, had been quite enough, thank you very much. These folks play for keeps, and keeps usually means that someone dies. Two already had, in this case, and I was certain our digging would bring the mob's focus directly onto me.

OK, that's not a problem; I had been a target before. But in those cases, my teenage son wasn't standing beside me. I had let Paulo help out with this case because I wanted him to get hooked on the art of private investigation so that when the time was right, he could join the business. I also thought this case was benign. After all, what could happen in a parking garage?

Paulo had dug up most of the clues we had so far and was again beaming from ear to ear. He was doing good investigative work and knew it. And so did I. But this case had just become very dangerous. I knew how to handle these "guys from Jersey." But I couldn't put my son at risk.

"Let's go back to the office and figure out our next move," I told Paulo. Maybe I could come up with something during the ride back. We were both very quiet. I could imagine that Paulo was thinking the same thing I was and coming up with a list of reasons why he should stay on the case. We got to the office and I called my wife, office manager, best friend and Paulo's mother, Shirley, into the office. It wasn't crowded. They were all the same person. I figured I could use some backup.

I was about to begin my speech, which I was handily composing on the spot, when Paulo held up his hand. The next five minutes made me the proudest parent on the face of the Earth.

"I've been thinking," he started.

"These mob guys can be pretty dangerous. I know you can handle them, but I don't have a lot of experience. I would hate for you to get hurt because I was there and you were protecting me instead of yourself.

"Why don't we divide the case into two parts? First, there is the field work; you can do that. And then there's the research and follow-up; I can do that. I'll work here with Mom, and you and I can discuss the case every day and update each other on new developments. I can think about the problem, and you can go out and get the clues. We'll make a great team."

There were tears in my eyes when Paulo finished. I couldn't have said it better. Shirley just smiled, got up and left the room. She knew her son a lot better than I knew mine. But I was learning fast.

After we did some male stuff (the teenage equivalent of "how 'bout them Dodgers") to give me a chance to wipe my eyes, I suggested we make a list of what we had discovered thus far, and then look for the obvious next step.

The current owners of the garage had contracted a consulting firm to test it for problems (it was this process that created what we thought were ghosts and got us into the case). Two employees of the firm had been murdered at the job site. We found that when the garage was being built, the mob was at least peripherally involved. The builder-owner was very nervous when we asked about the garage, and it was his wife who led us to the identity of original property owners—Palermo Ltd., the mob.

It seemed that the consulting firm was just in the wrong place at the wrong time. All except for one part: Paulo's idea that something had been put into the garage when the concrete was wet, something its owners didn't want found. As the consultant's engineers were dragging chains across the floor, they would have been able to hear where the rebar in the concrete was rusting. They would also be able to tell where something might be that shouldn't be there. Jimmy Hoffa? I don't think so. But what?

We decided we needed to know more about the operation. I was reluctant to go back to the consultants, Segal and Straer. They were in mourning because two of their own, including the local branch manager, had been killed. Paulo suggested that perhaps he could do some research on the phone, while I followed up with a call to Bill Vose. I asked Bill to join me for a drink at a watering hole called The Badge. It was near Parker Center, LAPD headquarters, and was frequented by cops of all ranks. On the way, I stopped off at Trader Joe's and picked up a bottle of 20-year-old Glenfiddich. I could pay my (actually, Paulo's) debt for the information Bill gave Paulo earlier in this case.

Bill was a few minutes late. I didn't mind. I liked the bar. It was a man's bar, although many female cops put a foot on the brass rail. And The Badge had a great selection of Scotch whisky. I ordered a shot of Isle of Jura, a nice little single-malt, and was adding just the right amount of water (a dollop) when Bill walked in.

He was accompanied by a man whose clothes, demeanor and walk said one thing: FBI.

Bill introduced me to the Special Agent in Charge of the Los Angeles FBI Office, William Harris. They ordered their drinks, and we took a booth.

Harris got right to the point. “We would like you and your firm to stop working the garage murders case. Tell your client whatever you want, but back off. This is much bigger than you or even the LAPD.”

I could see that Bill didn’t like the last sentence, but he didn’t say a word.

“Why?” I said, in wonderful detective repartee.

“Because if you continue, you could get killed.”

I drank the rest of my whisky and said nothing.

8

THE CONTENTS WERE WORTH HIS LIFE...

I left my friend LAPD Capt. Bill Vose and the FBI agent in the bar and went back to my car. The agent would give me no further information on the case except the potential for my demise. This wasn't going to work. I don't give up based on some bureaucrat's orders, even if he was the Special Agent in Charge of the FBI's LA office.

I called my office and asked Paulo what he'd found in his research on garage construction and repair. He said he had some interesting news. He had spoken to a consultant who knew "everything" about garages and was willing to come by the office that afternoon. He told Paul he was surprised the 30-year-old garage was in such bad shape that it needed so much work.

Dick Richards was sitting in my office with Paulo when I got there.

"That was quick," I said. Paulo made the introductions.

"Well, I went over to the garage and took a look around," Richards said. "Here's the deal. The kind of problem they are looking for usually happens in 'rust belt' or 'snow belt' areas, or near the beach. This garage is in Southern California. There is no snow, ice or salt, and relatively few big swings in temperature. In addition, wet, salty air, like you would find in Miami or Houston, isn't a factor—this deck is five miles from the nearest body of water.

"Plus, I walked the floors, and there are no visible signs of disrepair," Richards said. "Usually you see some cracking or concrete crumbling. This place is pristine. The owners must have taken good care of it. I even noticed that the membrane looked new."

"Membrane?" I asked.

"Yeah, they usually don't just pour the concrete but add a thin chemical coating to protect the deck. This must be replaced every five-to-10 years. Most garages don't do this, and that's where you get into trouble. This garage had normal maintenance and membrane replacement done right on schedule. It seems they are spending a lot of money checking something that doesn't need to be checked."

"The new owner told us he was rather ambivalent over the garage," I said. "They might keep it, or they might tear it down and put up a mid-rise. There's a lot of new construction in the area. It does seem strange to spend so much money on testing."

"Unless," said Paulo, "they were looking for something. I think there's a question we need to ask the new owner."

We thanked Richards for his input, and I left Paulo to his research and drove over to the Westside offices of S and J Investments.

Ray Schumer saw me immediately. "Well, Manning, cracked the case yet?"

"We're getting close, but I need a bit more information from you. How did you come to do the tests on the garage?"

"Let's see. After the deal closed, we got a call from Deswal Consulting recommending that we test the garage for structural problems. We thought it was overkill, but they gave us such a good price we could hardly say no."

"Oh, one more question, Ray. Was there any publicity about your purchase of the garage?"

"Well, sure. Our PR folks put a blurb in the trade papers. It was good publicity. We were hoping we might get a 'nibble' by a major firm to lease a new building. If not, we could keep the facility as a garage until we found a tenant."

I called Paulo and had him phone Deswal's main office in Cleveland. I told him the questions to ask. By the time I got back to my office, that toothy grin was on his face. He had the poop.

"I spoke to the regional manager for Deswal. He told me the entire firm was stricken by the murders of the two engineers here in California," Paulo said. "I asked him if he had been in contact with the owners and he said no, that their customer wasn't the owner but a company that told them it wanted to purchase the garage and needed testing conducted first. That company was 'Palermo Ltd.' "

Paulo made the next call, and I drove over to the Southern California office of Deswal in Burbank. The new manager, Martina Smithson, recently promoted on the murder of her predecessor, was waiting for me. Paulo and I had spoken to her on our previous visit.

I went right for it. "OK, let's cut the crap." I just love that detective talk.

"I know that Deswal wasn't hired by the owners but by another outfit with a foreign-sounding name. I know that you misled the current owner and gave him a bargain-basement price because, I assume, your client wanted you to take a quiet look into the garage.

"I also know that you were aware that the garage really didn't need a survey, probably told your client that, and they said do it anyway. I also am pretty sure that just before the work started, you, or your recently deceased boss, were paid a visit by a couple of big guys with bulges under their suits and that a lot of money changed hands.

"You were told to look for something buried in the garage and call them when you found it. How am I doing so far?"

Smithson had turned very pale. "Actually, one of them was short."

"Oh, but when your boss and his co-worker found the 'item,' they dug it up and decided to up the ante and were killed for their trouble."

"OK, you're right. Frank and Charlie tried to get more out of Palermo, and they were killed. But they didn't get the box."

"Box, what box?"

"The box they found in the garage. The two goons think I'm a secretary and didn't pay me any mind. But Frank told me the story when he heard that Charlie had been killed. He had hidden the box and was killed before he could tell me where he'd left it."

"What was in it?"

"All Frank told me was that when they opened the box, the papers inside were worth a hell of a lot more to some people than the measly 50 grand they had paid him and Charlie. I guess he was right. It was worth his life.

"The only clue was this key."

She handed me the key to a locker. "I don't know what it unlocks."

I looked on the back of the key and saw the outline of a familiar building. I told her I would take it from there.

I drove 20 minutes downtown to Union Station.

The famed terminal was built in 1939 to resemble one of Father Sierra's missions, on steroids. It was a combination of early California mission-style and art deco. Its location across from Olvera Street, the birthplace of Los Angeles, was no accident. Political forces came into play to ensure the plaza and surrounding buildings were protected.

As I walked quickly past the oversized leather seats in the main lobby I noticed two rather large gentlemen in dark suits shadowing me as they moved alongside the walls. I decided it was time for a cup of coffee and to rethink my next move.

I stood at the coffee bar and had an idea. I found a small side room off the main lobby. It was empty. I strolled in and the two came in right behind me. I turned quickly and tossed the coffee in the eyes of the one on the left. At the same time I ground my heel into the instep of the one on the right. I grabbed the one with the coffee baptism and pulled his arm behind his back just a tad too far. A quick pop told me he was out of the game.

I ministered to the other's foot one more time and heard a couple of bones break.

The lockers were only a few steps away. I put in the key and turned it. It was as empty as Mother Hubbard's cupboard.

9

The Story Begins to Make Sense... Well, Kinda

Time to call in the cavalry. I phoned Vose and told him it was time for another meeting. He said he would contact the FBI and be at my office in an hour. They were there in 30 minutes.

I thought if I rehashed the case from the beginning, it would give us a good place to start.

Not for long, as everyone started talking at once. All the sentences were questions, and they were all directed at me.

"OK, OK," I said. "Let's calm down. Obviously, I have been lied to, and there is one person guilty of those lies. Martina Smithson, newly installed manager at the consulting firm doing the work at the garage, and former assistant to the man who found the box and paid with his life for doing so.

"I have established a relationship with her," I told them. "Let me go over and talk to her. This time, she will tell me the truth."

I got a lecture from the FBI Special Agent in Charge for Los Angeles about overstepping my bounds, interfering with an ongoing investigation, and jail time. I was gratified when Bill took my side and stepped outside with the Feebie. When Bill returned, he was alone, drenched in sweat, and smiling. I was sure he had called in a few markers and taken a bit of abuse, but I had a free hand...for now.

I left immediately for the consulting firm's office in Burbank. When I arrived, I saw Smithson heading toward the hotel across from the office building. She was carrying an overnight bag. She stopped in front of the hotel and was waiting beside the sign that read, "Airport Shuttle." I walked over and stood beside her.

"You aren't going anywhere. Do you want to have the conversation here, in the coffee shop, in your office, in my office, or down at LAPD headquarters? Make no mistake; those are your only choices."

Tears welled up, and she said the coffee shop would be fine.

"So talk."

"First, Mr. Manning, I'm sorry I lied to you. I just didn't know what to do or who to trust. But now, I guess I have no choice. Frank told me where he put the key to the station locker, but he also told me what was in the box. Our relationship was a little closer than the usual boss/employee. I spent most of my evenings at his townhouse in the hills above Universal City.

"He told me where he had put the papers he found in the box. After he was killed, I took the papers to the safe at the office. I didn't know what else to do with them."

I was preparing to give Smithson another of my patented, "Well?" looks, when she continued.

"The box contained several documents. Frank had explained that this was a time capsule. One of the capo de capos back east was heavily involved in a lot of illegal deals with the FBI and the Justice Department during the Kennedy administration. The documents put not only the government but the election of JFK in a bad light.

"The capo had kept the documents to protect himself, but he was dying. J. Edgar Hoover knew he had the papers and put pressure on him to destroy them. The mobster made a big deal of burning them in front of a bunch of government bigwigs. But he burned only copies.

"He wanted to hide them where they couldn't be found for years. He had some 'contacts' with a parking firm in New York

City, and they told him about the garage being built in Los Angeles. The capo had his most trusted lieutenant take the box with the documents and bury it in the wet concrete and then stay to watch while it dried."

"How do you know all this?" I asked Smithson.

"A letter included with the documents explained what happened. The capo de capo was, along with his other interests, was a history buff. He wanted future generations to know what had gone on in the early 1960s. And that's the story."

I could understand why, when the Mob heard that the garage might be torn down, they had to find that box and were willing to pay to get it. However, when Frank, Smithson's boss, tried to hold them up for more, they killed him but didn't wind up with the box.

I could also understand why a certain family in Boston and the FBI might want to keep the knowledge in those documents off the Internet and out of the press.

"So where are the papers now?" I asked Smithson.

"I have them in my purse."

Oh, please. Nothing was as simple as that. All we had to do was walk out, get in my car, place a call to...to...to whom?

The FBI certainly was not at the top of the list. And who knows what kind of deal Vose and the LAPD cut? Best friends only go so far. The Mob wasn't on my speed dial, and frankly, I wouldn't be getting Christmas cards from the two enforcers I had laid out when I got the box from the locker at the bus station.

I could call my friend at the LA Times, but what if this was all a bunch of hooey. The documents could be legit, or they could be another hoax. We would be destroying reputations, families, and altering history. They would have to rename a thousand high schools, and a couple of colleges.

Simplicity just flew out the window.

Then I had an idea. I told Smithson to give me the documents and continue with her travel plans. She would probably be safe in Cabo or wherever she was going. I told her to call me when she got settled and I would let her know when it was safe to come home.

I walked her back to the shuttle stop and watched as she rode off to the Hollywood Burbank airport.

When I got to my car, I pulled off the inner door covering and slipped the documents inside. They would have to search the car thoroughly to find them. As I drove out of the parking lot, I noticed a Mob-mobile in my rearview mirror. Perfect. That's exactly what I wanted.

I turned into a residential neighborhood and gave them the chance to cut me off. Two gunsels jumped out of their car and ran over to mine. Their movements told me they weren't connected with the two I had met at the bus station (and had left in traction).

One of them jerked me out of my car and took me to theirs. As we drove off, I noticed the other one behind us, following in my car.

I had been kidnapped once before by the boys from Salerno, and they had covered my head so that when they turned me loose, I couldn't tell anyone where I had been.

They didn't take that precaution this time. Not a good sign. I was beginning to think that I hadn't thought this bright idea through.

10

Endgame

We drove to Beverly Hills, the "poor" section south of Wilshire. A few offices and a lot of apartments on this side of town. The car stopped in front of a building likely built in the '50s. It was a Colonial, painted white with blue trim. Impatiens filled the flower boxes. A brass plaque next to the door read, "Commonwealth Investigations."

Hold it, this didn't sound like the Mob to me.

I was taken out of the car, and we walked into the building and down a long hallway. I could see offices to the left and right. They were inhabited by smart-looking men and women, all of whom seemed to be busy at computer terminals. Ahead was an open door, and I could see people sitting around a conference table.

The room was apportioned like a movie set. Mahogany walls, a thick gray carpet on the floor. A full complement of audio and video equipment had been discretely placed in the walls. I noted one of those three-legged speakerphones in the center of the table.

I looked around the table and was beginning to understand.

To my right was the special agent in charge of the FBI's Los Angeles office; to my left was my "best friend," Bill Vose of the LAPD. Next to Bill was my contact, Martina Smithson, and across from her was my son, Paul Junior. Next to Paulo was Rick Johnson, the man who originally built that garage where the documents were buried in 1968. Johnson's tennis-playing wife sat next to him.

I realized that with the exception of Paulo, everyone in the room knew the contents of the box. I sat down at the head of the table.

FBI agent William Harris started by glaring at me and yelling. "For Pete's sake, Manning, see the mess you have caused? We had this under control and then you stuck your nose in, and now we're trying to contain a nightmare. I'm going to throw every book I can find at you."

At that moment, a voice came from the speakerphone. "You aren't throwing anything, Mr. Harris. Why don't you keep quiet and let's see what we can do about our mutual problem."

The voice was rich and full. It was a voice that was easily recognizable. Its Boston Brahmin accent was unmistakable. I had heard it on the news many times. I had watched his speeches at political conventions. He had lived a celebrated, and difficult life. And recent headlines told me that he was now attempting to protect his legacy, and that of his very famous family, and he didn't have a lot of time.

"Mr. Manning, I'm sure you know who I am, so there's no need for introductions. To clear up one issue first: You are not a prisoner. I had you brought here by members of Commonwealth's staff because I need your help.

"Your assumption is correct. Everyone who knows what is in those documents is in this room. Your son is here because he is involved, and in time would uncover our little secret.

"I was young, and as you know, not very bright when the incidents documented in those papers transpired. I'm not proud of what happened, and I'm sure that if they were here, the rest of my family wouldn't be either. I wasn't personally involved; I had troubles of my own. However, I know for an absolute certainty that what they were doing was in the best interests of this country.

"They inherited a snake pit in Washington. The FBI was out of control. Relationships that were, let's say, 'questionable,' as was the order of the day. The Soviets were rattling nukes; missiles were 90 miles from our shores. It was a very difficult time.

"Yet, they were and are loved by Americans and people around the world.

"I know for a fact that they were beginning to clean up the problems in their administration. The documents were used to blackmail them into going slow. As you know, they ran out of time in November 1963.

"A certain gentleman held the documents to keep the government at bay for five years. Finally, as he neared his death, he agreed to destroy them. He didn't, and here we are today.

"Frankly, I don't know where to go from this point. I have used my influence to gain the assistance of the FBI and through them the LAPD. Mr. and Mrs. Johnson, as well as the others present, have graciously agreed to anything you and I decide.

"I guess that means it's now up to you, Mr. Manning."

The last sentence hung in the air, and everyone looked at me. It was time for some famous Manning wisdom. Damn, I wished I had some.

"What about the two deaths at the garage?" I said.

"There were two parties involved in the search for the documents; the murders were done by the gentlemen you colorfully noted as originating from a southern Mediterranean country. They are under arrest at the medical center where you so competently placed them. I understand that their employers have bowed out of the matter and will no longer be involved."

"Why don't you just take the documents, burn them and that will be the end of it?" I asked.

He cleared his throat. "There has been enough subterfuge. That's what got us into this mess in the first place. We need good people to come to an honorable solution."

He had done his homework. He knew that, once given, I wouldn't go back on my word.

"How's this?" I said. "I will lock the documents in a safe deposit box. Two keys will be required to open it. One I will keep; the other you can keep. I can speak only for my son and myself, but we will agree to never mention this to anyone outside this room, ever.

"If you want the documents released," I said, "you can notify me. I understand you may have some time constraints, so if you like, you can name another party to hold your key."

"Well, Mr. Manning, you do live up to your reputation. It is agreed. We won't be speaking again. I wish you all the best."

The red light on the speakerphone went off. Silence filled the room.

I looked at Paulo and nodded toward the door. He got up and I followed him out. We retrieved my car and I pulled the documents out from the side panel of the door. We headed for the main branch of our bank; it was just around the corner on Doheny Drive. I noticed a car following close behind. We parked in front of the bank, and the car drove by and turned left. We didn't see it again.

It took only a few minutes to set up the account. I signed the cards and Paulo signed for the second key. It was understood access would be granted as long as two people and two keys were present.

I then drove to the local FedEx office, placed a key into an envelope along with one of my business cards, and sent it to an address in Washington, D.C. I checked the box that required only one person to sign for the letter.

Paulo and I hadn't said a word since we left the conference room. We drove back to the office. Bill Vose of the LAPD was sitting there with a bottle of 16-year-old Ardbeg. It was open, and at least one shot had been poured and consumed.

Bill said, "Sorry, Paul, the FBI had me between a rock and a hard place."

I looked at my friend and considered all that had happened in the last three hours. I poured a drink for both of us.

"I don't agree with anything that man has done," I said, "but he showed some class today."

We drank silently for a moment.

Then Paulo said to Bill: "The Ardbeg goes a long way toward getting you off the hook."

My son is going to make a great detective.

Episode Three

The Rendezvous

1

Time Flies When You Are Having Fun

Time flies when you are having fun, and boy, have I been having fun. The last 40 years went by in a flash. It's a new century. LA has grown, and my business is booming. Wow! With Shirley running the office, and Jim Walsh coming over from the Bel Air patrol, we were able to build a reputation. And it's a good one.

Yes, I did it, I married Shirley, and Paul Junior arrived a few years later. They tell me he's my spitting image, and I guess he is. He was raised in the detective business, helped out on stakeouts, and once when he was 15 he solved a case all by himself. Talk about a proud poppa.

He's out of the service, having served as a Marine in Desert Storm (I guess the jarheads are OK, now that my son is one) and has come back to work with dad. Just in time, too. All those long nights, a lack of exercise, and bad diet caught up with me and the doc said that I had to slow down or die. He's subtle, my doc.

So, the time is right. I'm closing in on 70, don't want to retire, so the partnership is perfect. I can keep my fingers in the pie; Junior can do the work, and benefit from my wisdom and experience. Maybe Shirley and I can take that cruise we've delayed since the parking caper that put Paul Manning on the map.

I single-handedly, with Shirley's and Jim's help, oh, yes, and the LAPD and Bel Air patrol, but who's counting, took out a dame who was running the local mob and solved a murder in a parking garage, plus discovered a money-laundering operation.

I also discovered that Shirley was my one true love. I think it was when she threw the vase of flowers in my lap at the hospital that tipped me off.

The publicity from the parking caper was terrific. I couldn't handle all the calls and asked for her help. She jumped at the chance to keep a closer eye on me and moved into my office a month later. She also told me that if we were going to continue our relationship, I had to marry her. Seemed reasonable at the time. And still does.

Business was so good I couldn't keep up and asked Jim Walsh to come work for me. He considered it for, oh, ten seconds and gave Capt. Hankins at Bel Air his notice. We didn't burn any bridges (I asked the Captain's approval before approaching Jim). His group with all its contacts was an invaluable referral.

We moved to new offices on Sunset Boulevard. It was a Spanish-style single-story building with ample space. My office has a great view of the strip and the constant parade on the sidewalk outside. I figured we could rent out some of the space and then grow into it. Being on the Sunset Strip was a good location for getting around town.

We were about 20 minutes from police headquarters downtown, 15 minutes from the Valley (via Laurel Canyon or Beverly Glen), and about 20 minutes from the beach cities. And we didn't have to take the freeways.

I have seen this city grow from a segregated mess ruled by the iron fist of the LAPD to the most diverse and cosmopolitan city on earth. The cops are pros now and treat everyone like human beings, sort of. Much of the diversity is Latin, with so-called "Spanish surname" folks, legal and illegal, making up over half the population. But the Koreans, Iranians, Vietnamese, Japanese, Chinese, Jews, Canadians, French, and the rest add a wonderful mix of cultures and languages. Los

Angeles is a bazaar of diversity. You can find anything here, get anything here, and if you aren't careful, get into trouble here.

That's where we come in. We help people who are in trouble. And hopefully, help them out of it. All they have to do is call "Paul Manning and Son, Investigations."

Junior had just finished up a case and was in his office with the client to, at least I hoped, collect our final check, when Shirley announced someone in the outer office waiting to see "Mr. Manning."

"Junior or Senior?" I asked.

"Based on the age of the potential client, Junior, but Pauly is busy, so it's over to you."

She stepped aside and the most beautiful woman I had ever seen (except Shirley, of course) walked through the door. She was blonde, perfectly proportioned, and carried herself like a lady. Shirley gave me a look that said, "Hands off, Tiger," and closed the door.

I stood and put out my hand—"Paul Manning." A look of confusion crossed her face.

"I, I, I, I'm Grace Lundquist," she stuttered. My unerring detective skills, honed with a half-century of experience, told me she was expecting my son. "I'm sorry, Mr. Manning," she managed. "I just thought you'd be…younger."

I laughed and said, "You were expecting my son, Paul. He's busy, and I'm to keep you company until he finishes." The look of relief on her face didn't do much for my ego, but this wasn't the first time it happened.

At that moment, Paul walked in. He was a duplicate of me 35 years ago. Tall, rock-solid, handsome, and smart. He was definitely his own man, so I enjoy giving him a little jab now and then. "Junior, this is Grace Lundquist." He gave me a look that brought back memories of a landlord in my first case years ago. He didn't like being called "Junior," particularly in front of a client.

"Miss Lundquist," he said, shaking her hand and sitting in the empty chair next to hers. "How can we help you?"

"I work in one of those buildings on Olympic Boulevard, just west of the 405. My office overlooks a parking garage. I can see the roof and am certain something funny is going on. I know you must think I'm crazy, but every day about the same time, two cars come up to the roof—it's usually empty—and something is passed between them, and then they both leave."

"Have you tried reporting this to the police?" asked Paul.

"They were polite but I think they were too busy for my-off-the-wall observations. So yesterday I hid behind the elevator to watch. The cars arrived but one of the men saw me and started toward me. I ran down the stairwell and escaped, but I think he saw me enter my building. I'm afraid he may come after me. I spoke to the security director in the building and he recommended your services."

At that moment, a shot came through my office window and struck Grace in the chest. She hit the floor like a sack of wet cement.

2

But Do We Still Have A Client?

I was accustomed to seeing people shot during my year in Iraq in Desert Storm, but it was a shock to have it happen in Dad's office. I was on her almost before the sound of the gun stopped reverberating and administered aid—clear the air passages, stop the bleeding, and treat for shock. Mom came running through the door and told us she had called 911. Dad grabbed his gun from the desk and jumped over to the side window and peered out.

"Don't see anything except a black Towncar heading east toward La Cienega, and a couple of people who hit the deck when they heard the shot," he said. "How's Grace?"

"She's still breathing, but just barely," I said. "I'm putting pressure on the wound, but paramedics would help about now." Sirens in the background answered that request. We were only three minutes from Cedars-Sinai Medical Center, and judging by the color of Grace's face, that was a good thing.

Cedars Sinai has a first-rate trauma and emergency center. Its surgeons were trained in 'Nam and Iraq. They know gunshot wounds and how to fix them. The ER was an armed camp, with bulletproof glass, automatic doors requiring cards, and every other protective measure. An armed guard with a dog stood in the waiting room at all times. Seems gangbangers liked to follow-up to ensure the success of their handiwork.

Jim Walsh came running in as paramedics were loading Grace on the fold-up stretcher, readying her for the ambulance.

"What the hell is going on? Is everyone OK?" We assured him it was all under control. Jim is our partner. He saved Dad's life in the parking business caper that put Paul Manning, Investigations on the map before I was born. Jim came to work with Dad a few months later. Jim is my godfather; we have an "uncle-nephew" relationship.

I grew up in the detective business, and came to work with Dad, Mom and Jim after I left the Marines. I was made partner, and the name on the door became, "Paul Manning and Son, Investigations."

So we had a case; I just hoped we still had a client. Jim had to be brought up-to-date. I figured he would grasp the gist of it soon enough as a pair of cops strolled through the door with that, "Don't anybody leave town," look in their eyes.

We knew them fairly well. Dad was a former LAPD officer, and we often worked with the police. What I found strange was that these cops were from the L.A. County Sheriff's Department. Sunset Strip isn't in Los Angeles, although it is surrounded by LA. The Strip is in West Hollywood, which contracts with the Sheriff's Department for its policing. It's the largest sheriff's department in the world, and with 8,600 officers, it's only slightly smaller than the LAPD itself. The Sheriff's Department provides police services for more than 40 communities in the county, plus its unincorporated areas.

West Hollywood is typical L.A. It's a district of gays and retirees who, about 15 years ago, had some common problems (discrimination, health issues, insurance, to name a few), so they banded together and formed a city from a long narrow strip roughly paralleling Santa Monica Boulevard, just south and west of Hollywood proper. Its almost 2 square miles is an eclectic mix of art, film, restaurants, and tony shops and markets.

I once asked my macho dad his feelings about the gay population. He said he had many friends in the community and was saddened by the plague that ravaged it. He wished more could be done, but knew, as with most problems unique to a community, the solution would come from within as much as from without. He then abruptly changed the subject. It was one of the few times I saw a tear in my father's eye.

But the cops in our office weren't there for a travelogue. Wil Murray—"Lt. Murray," to most—was leading the investigation. He tried to be gruff, but found it hard to pull off since he'd also attended my fifth birthday party. From what I understand my dad and "Uncle" Jim went out on the deck with Wil while we kids were playing in the house to "test" a bottle of 18-year-old Macallam. The results of that test had been kept from me for more than three decades.

I told Bill that Grace Lundquist was given our name as a referral and she feared she had been followed. It seemed she had witnessed some rendezvous on the roof of the parking garage outside her Olympic Boulevard office building. She was about to tell us more when she was shot. "I guess she was right about the being-followed part," quipped Dad.

Wil told us a quick check of the partial Dad got on the Towncar's license plates led to a '95 Taurus registered in the Valley. It was a dead end. I only hoped Grace wasn't one too.

The hospital called about an hour later. Grace was out of surgery and resting comfortably. No major organs were hit, and the pressure I had put on the wound helped keep most of her blood where it belonged. We could talk to her in a day or so.

Now what? Wil and his partner left with the admonition that we should let them know if we heard anything new. This was a sticky case for them as it crossed jurisdictions—Olympic Boulevard being in L.A. proper—but he was certain the Sheriff's Department could work it out with the LAPD.

In the meantime, Dad, Jim and I discussed our next move. I was going to Grace's office building on Olympic, Jim would work the Towncar angle, and Dad would call in a few chips he had with the Sheriff's Department crime lab to see if they could get forensics off the bullet.

That all changed with the ringing of the phone; it was Wil at the hospital. Someone had broken through the ER security and shot up Grace's recovery room. There were people down. The shooter got away in a black Towncar. We jumped in my jeep and headed for Cedars.

3

A Voice I Hadn't Heard In…

It was only about a three-minute ride down La Cienega to Cedars-Sinai. Paulo made it in two. When we turned the corner onto Beverly and pulled up at the hospital ER, I was certain we were going to be its next customer. Jeeps have a high center of gravity. Paulo was grinning as we stopped short of the yellow tape.

There were police from three jurisdictions—the LAPD and the Sheriff's Department, and Beverly Hills was directing traffic. We were literally a couple of blocks from their turf. Choppers whirred overhead bearing the names of local radio and TV stations. This was going to rival the O.J. Simpson low-speed chase.

Fortunately, Wil was standing outside and waved us through the line.

"Sorry to have overreacted on the phone," he said. "The security guys here were great. Oh, the bad guy got some shots off, but the dog handler turned loose his shepherd, Goldie. The shooter took one look at those teeth and headed for the door.

"The 'people down' was just about everyone in the area who hit the deck when they heard the shots. No one was injured, but my guess is that the hood with the gun may have a problem where the dog took a piece out of his leg."

With a sigh of relief, Paulo and I went back to the car and regrouped. We decided the plan of action we had devised before the phone call was still good. We called Shirley, and she let Jim know that he should get moving on tracking down the Towncar. Paulo would sniff around Grace's office and the parking garage. He would leave me here where I would learn I could about the shooter and talk to Bill about any evidence that may have been uncovered.

I know, I know—this was a police matter and we are private. But nobody, I mean nobody shoots a client in my office and gets away with it. Bill Murray was going to have his hands full negotiating with the LAPD. This was becoming a big case. Grace was shot in West Hollywood, under the purview of the L.A. County sheriff. Cedars-Sinai, the scene of the latest shootout, was in the city of Los Angeles. Grace's office was in L.A. too. The main question would be who wanted the publicity. As long as it was good, everyone wanted it. But if it went sour—there'd be no sign of a public relations officer anywhere.

Since the LAPD might not look too good with a major hospital emergency room shot up right under its nose, I thought they might just let the Sheriff's Department take the case. Boy, was I wrong.

The news conference was already set up. It looked as if some movie star was being perp-walked after confessing to having a working girl in his Maserati. There were dozens of satellite trucks, choppers and slick-looking reporters. Men and women doing a "standup" to find a spin that would put their piece on the nightly news in New York, with the chance of a promotion thrown into the mix.

The LAPD was everywhere and organizing the press like you would a stampede. It was fun to watch. Commander Bill Vose held up his hands in a plea, or was it a prayer, for quiet. I had known Bill forever. He had been my partner at the LAPD and later my boss when I was fired from the force. He had tried to protect me, but it wasn't in the cards. We kept in touch, and have remained good friends. Bill had worked his way up through the department and now was a head honcho downtown. He was the "go-to" person when something big was happening and the press needed a statement. Judging by his involvement, this just might be bigger than I thought.

Bill tried to placate the reporters, to no avail. They wanted something, and he had nothing. Finally, he told them there would be a full report and press conference the next day downtown. I caught his eye as he left the microphones.

He came over and shook my hand. "I should have known you would be involved in this mess," Bill said with a smile. "Here we have a complicated turf war starting, an unknown shooter or shooters, a wounded witness to who knows what, and you and your kid are in the middle of it."

"Now wait just a minute, Bill. We were simply doing our jobs. It's not our fault someone wanted our client dead. Frankly, we don't know anything more than you do; besides, the Sheriff's deputies have the lead on this, not you."

"Well, our brass just spoke to the sheriff, and he graciously handed it over to us," Bill said, again with the smile. "And I now have a first: I have information before you do."

"What? Give!" I put my hand on his lapel. Bill and I are very close, which is fortunate because most cops don't like being touched, particularly by a PI.

"OK, OK, calm down," he said. "It's getting late and I'm going off-duty. Let's go across the street to Morton's and have a drink."

Morton's wasn't exactly a cop bar. It was part of a chain of high-end steakhouses and fit well into the trendy area where West Hollywood, L.A. and Beverly Hills met. They had good single-malts and a decent lounge where we could talk.

Bill ordered an 18-year-old Glenlivet. As a whisky, it's not spectacular, but it's taken me nearly 30 years to wean him off Maker's Mark. I felt perverse and had a Laphroaig with a splash of water. We took a couple of minutes to enjoy our drinks and then Bill began.

"We aren't sure, but we think this may have something to do with union organizing."

"What?" I said. "Unions? In a parking lot? I can't believe it. Why would someone want to organize a parking attendant?"

"I don't know much about it," Bill said. "It's being handled by our organized crime division. However, I do know that the deck next to your client's building is one of the first to be organized in the city. I don't think the legitimate unions are involved, but this one seems to have close ties to Vegas and New Jersey."

This is where I came in. That first case years ago was about the Mob and parking and money laundering. A greedy "businessman" who owned a parking operation, as well as other interests, had used the lots to launder money that he made illegally in numbers and the rackets.

The East Coast wise guys had set up a beautiful Italian woman, a "B-movie" actress and onetime flame of Howard Hughes, to take over the parking operation. I stumbled into the middle of it and with unerring detective skills, plus a lot of luck, stopped the flow of ill-gotten gain. I hadn't thought about parking, except as a place to put my car, in nearly four decades.

"Wow," I said, "those guys can play rough. I thought the parking business had been clean for years."

"The parking business itself is," Bill said. And he left it at that.

I paid the bill and called Jim Walsh to come pick me up. As I waited, I began to worry that Paulo might be walking into a hornet's nest. I called his cellphone and it kicked into voicemail. I called Shirley, and she hadn't heard from him. This was unusual. He always checked in when he left an interview.

As I was fretting, my phone rang. I thought I recognized the Southern European accent—a voice soft as moonlight dancing on the Spanish Steps in Rome, but clear as the howl of a wolf on the slopes of Mt. Etna.

"So, Mr. Paul Manning, you are sticking your nose into my business again. This time, you and your son—Paul Junior, isn't it—won't be so lucky." The phone went dead.

4

My Questions Get Attention

I was feeling pretty good as I left Dad at Cedars-Sinai Medical Center. Grace was not in danger, and no one had been hurt in the follow-up shooting in the ER. I headed over to Grace's office on Olympic to do some first-class detecting. It was about a 15-minute drive, down Robertson to a right on Olympic, through Century City, past the 405 and on to the so-called Olympic Corridor.

Century City is a designer complex with residential high-rise condos, retail shopping and restaurants built on the back lot of Fox Studios. Alcoa Aluminum was one of the partners in the project, and they say that if you look straight down at the development from above, the matching 44-story triangular-shaped theme towers form the familiar Alcoa logo. If you are anybody in the media or related in the legal profession in L.A., your office is in Century City.

The Olympic Corridor is the "second Century City" on L.A.'s west side. There are about half-a-dozen relatively new mid-rise office buildings, with some second-tier media, financial and service companies. It's a modern section of L.A., but has a rich history.

Around the turn of the century, Japanese immigrants settled there and planted lush gardens throughout the area. Even today, you can see some in overgrown backyards, with the quiet art of the gardener mixed with the ruin of Mother Nature. However, WWII and the subsequent internment took its toll, and when the residents returned, most of their properties were gone. They resettled in the area, however, and

Sawtelle Boulevard, which bisects Olympic, has become home to Japanese nurseries and sake and sushi bars.

I drove into the parking structure next to Grace's building and went up to the roof. It was empty, but I did note that you could walk directly from the office building onto the roof of the garage, and the entire roof was visible from the offices on that side of the tower. Grace had told my dad and me, just before the shot was fired, that she had seen suspicious activity up there—two cars coming up to the roof daily, something changing hands, and then both leaving. I had thought drugs, but who knows?

I went down to the building office and asked for the security director; he had recommended our firm to Grace when the LAPD hadn't expressed much interest in her story. I wasn't surprised to recognize an old friend.

The law enforcement community is a small one. And even though I was new in it, Dad's contacts and the fact that I grew up working cases with him meant I knew a lot of folks, including retired Santa Monica Deputy Police Chief Bill Shannon.

Outsiders think of L.A. as one big city, but in reality, it is comprised of many smaller communities with their own police departments, such as Beverly Hills, Culver City, El Segundo, Manhattan Beach, Torrance and, of course, Santa Monica. Senior officers who retired after 30 years were in demand, particularly by property management companies, to serve as heads of security. Bill was one of them.

"Hi, Paul," Shannon said. "I thought you or your dad would be showing up soon. I heard about the OK Corral activity at Cedars. Everybody OK?"

"Yes, Bill. No injuries, but I think Bill Vose was under attack. He was heading the LAPD press response team. Dad took him for a drink while I came over to check with you."

It's always best to give your seniors the lead. I was still considered a pup by most of the enforcement officers in the area. I had quickly learned to defer to them. We settled into Shannon's basement office, got coffee, and he began to talk.

"Grace told us she saw two cars showing up every day on the roof of the garage next-door. She was suspicious and, being a nosy gal, she went down to snoop around. When she did, she was spotted and chased but thought she had lost them. She must have been wrong."

"She came to me and I recommended that she call you two. I figured you had nothing better to do than squire a nice girl around town and test your white charger protecting the pure and innocent. I didn't think you would get her shot up."

That last line got my dander up. "For your information, bucko, we are on this like white on rice. Dad and I will nail the guys who shot her."

He held up his hands. "OK, OK, don't blow a gasket. You have your dad's temper and, I have to admit, his 'always-get-the-girl' looks. You know, I almost asked your mom out on a date before she married your dad. I guess the word 'almost' is why I'm still a bachelor."

"OK, peace. Now where do I go from here?"

Shannon leaned back in his chair. "Magnum Properties, the owner of this building and my employer, also owns the garage next-door. We have a private firm running the lot. It was built when the building was put up to meet the parking requirements set by the city.

"As usual, there is twice the number of spaces we need, and that top floor is always empty," he said. "The connecting walkway runs from our third floor to the third floor of the garage, next to the elevator tower. Grace's office is on the ninth floor, overlooking the garage roof.

"She is some graphic designer with Media Matters, the ad agency that just took over the Hollywood Bowl and Getty museum accounts," Shannon continued. "I think she does very well…just right for a guy like you."

Sheesh—Bill was trying to set me up. I guess my love life, or lack of it, was common knowledge among retired law enforcement. Enough of this; I had to get moving, over to the garage to see what I could find. I thanked Bill, told him I would keep him in the loop, and walked next door.

At the garage office, I spoke to a fellow who looked to be the manager.

"Hi, I'm Paul Manning. I'm a private investigator working on the shooting of Grace Lundquist. She parked in your garage. Can you tell me anything about her?"

He said nothing but entered something on his computer. "Grace Lundquist, $150 a month, works for Media Matters next-door, lives on Armacost, drives a 2003 Accord, 4ABC123. That's all I know. When was she shot?"

"Today. Mind if I look around?"

"No, go ahead, but I'm not sure what we have to do with that. This is just where she parked her car."

He printed out Grace's info and handed it to me. That in itself surprised me. As I walked out of the office, I thought I saw him reaching for his phone.

The garage had four levels, with about 200 spaces per level. It was, as Shannon had said, half full. Most of the cars were on the first and third levels—with easy access to the building next-door. I walked around to get the feel of the place. There appeared to be only two employees: the manager and the booth attendant at the exit. The sign said it was run by AB Parking. Where had I heard that before?

As I started back to my car, two of the biggest guys I had ever seen stepped out from behind a column. Obviously, my questions had come to someone's attention. I didn't hesitate for a second. I slammed my heel into the big one's instep, and he fell into the bigger one. I then kicked the bigger guy in his stomach, walked to my Jeep, drove carefully around the writhing bodies, paid my fee at the exit and left.

5

They Threaten My Shirley!

Jim Walsh picked me up at Cedars-Sinai Medical Center and we drove the short distance to the office. I thought about what I had learned over a whisky from my LAPD friend Bill Vose and the phone call with the voice from the past. Was Junior in trouble?

He arrived at the office five minutes later. I asked if he had any problems; he smiled and said there was an incident but no trouble.

"What do you mean, 'an incident'?"

"Well, we stirred up something, because as I left the garage, a couple of big bozos tried to rough me up. I used that trick you taught me a few years back," Paul Junior said.

"The instep and stomach routine?" I asked.

"Yep," he answered.

We then compared notes. The garage was run by AB Parking. That was the name of the company involved in our first case in the late '60s. I couldn't swear to it, but I thought the voice I heard on the phone belonged to Maria LaFlonza, the woman who had run the mob's takeover attempt of AB back then.

But it couldn't be her; she was in prison for murder, wasn't she? I asked Shirley to call Bill Vose. When she located him, I picked up the extension.

"Bill, is Maria LaFlonza still in Tehachapi?" I waited while he checked.

"She's been out 10 years—good behavior," Vose said.

"Well, she may have been on good behavior in prison, but she's back to her old tricks now." I filled Bill in on the phone call and Junior's parking garage incident.

"Do you want police protection?"

"No, that will scare them off. We'll handle it on this end."

With that, Vose went into a tirade about getting involved in police business, lying low, taking a long vacation, and then, realizing to whom he was talking, simply said to keep him informed, and hung up.

Shirley asked what we should do next. I said we needed to know more about the parking business and what was happening in Los Angeles. She said she knew just the person to call.

The next afternoon, Betty Beeson was sitting in my office. Shirley was there, too, but I think it was more as a chaperone than anything else.

Betty had been my client years ago during the original parking caper. She was night manager for a garage in a building Shirley ran. Betty had suspected a problem, got involved in a murder, and I helped her out and untangled the mess. She had been beautiful then—and still was—and very much a blonde.

Along the way, Betty had connected up with DC McGuire, a retired parking expert from New York, and they had teamed up to form a parking company in L.A. Last I heard, DC had passed away, but Betty was still going great guns. If anyone knew about parking in the City of Angels, it would be her.

"Gosh, Paul, it's been so long and you look so great." I smiled and nodded. With Shirley sitting there, I wasn't about to return the compliment. Instead, I filled Betty in on the case.

"That terrible LaFlonza woman is out of prison? She should have been given 'the chair.'"

I hesitated to tell Betty that the chair had gone out of style in California, replaced by "the needle."

Crime was down considerably in California, due primarily to the three-strikes law, which forced judges to put repeat criminals in jail. I don't know if it's a 90/10 rule, but it's close: 90% of the crime is done by 10% of the criminals. This case seemed to prove the point: LaFlonza was out and she hadn't missed a beat. She was right back to the same business, recidivism at its best.

We knew that LaFlonza had personally killed Betty's boss, Gilberto Quintana, and had ordered Art Ball, the president of AB Parking, terminated. However, clever lawyers and the her testifying to stabbing Gilbert in a lover's quarrel, and no proof she had actually ordered the Ball killing, meant that LaFlonza got off with life. And that resulted a much shorter sentence.

The point was moot, anyway. She was out and up to her old tricks. What I needed now was some inside info from Betty.

"Well, I am sort of on the periphery of this issue," she said. "So far we have not had any union problems, and frankly I don't know of any major outfits in LA. To be honest, I don't think the unions have anything to do with this. I would go further. It might have something to do with taxes.

"L.A. instituted a parking tax a number of years ago," Betty said. "It's a problem for legitimate operators like me, because some of the sleazier outfits don't report their total income and then don't pay the tax. That being the case, they can out-bid me every time. I am successful because we run such a clean operation; however, these guys are into the kickback business. That's what your client may have seen happening on the parking garage roof."

"But how would LaFlonza be involved?"

"Well," Betty said, "if she was back with AB and using the lower expense of not paying taxes to underbid competitors for new locations, then she would be paying off and skimming right and left. For all I know, she might be involved in kickbacks to owners or owner's reps.

"Of course, she wouldn't be involved directly. She would have a legitimate front man to handle day-to-day operations and deal with her customers. The 'owner' of AB Parking is William Francis Smith. He's quite a character. Knows everyone and cuts a wide swath through City Hall. He's on the boards of many of the owners groups and gives a lot of money to their favorite charities. AB is only one of his interests. Supposedly he owns a lot of property himself and has part-interest in a hotel/casino in Vegas."

"Then we start with him," I said.

We walked Betty to the office door, and Shirley said we would set up dinner within the next couple of weeks. It would be fun finding out just how well the little girl from Iowa had done over the past 35 years. I told Shirley I would lock up; she went home.

Junior left for his house near the beach. He said he would be dropping by the hospital that evening to look in on our client.

Shirley and I live just a few blocks from the house I owned when we met. It was up Laurel Canyon and further toward the bowl on Mulholland. I liked to drive up Nichols Canyon. It was curvy and steep, but offered great views.

When I arrived at the house, I took a moment to gaze at the vista of Los Angeles, from the desert to the sea. What a wonderful place. We had moved here about 20 years ago when the prices weren't yet over the moon. The payments were a struggle in the beginning, but business was booming, and we wanted the place bad.

Shirley's car was in the driveway. As I headed toward the front door, I noticed water under her car. There was a pool near the right front tire. I took a closer look and saw that the "water" was thick like brake fluid. The brake line had been cut, and not too long ago.

Shirley met me at the door. Her kiss told me nothing was wrong. But she never would have made it down the hill to work the next morning.

6

We Get a Reaction from William Francis Smith

I left Dad at the office and went to visit Grace in the hospital. I felt guilty that she had been shot while sitting in our office. Dad and I were committed to finding the shooter, but still, it couldn't inspire much confidence in a new client.

Grace was at Cedars-Sinai in a room with a police guard stationed outside. The LAPD posted one of its finest there after someone had shot up the emergency room trying to finish the job on Grace.

I walked in her room and she was sitting up. She looked rather pale, but she smiled and said: "Oh, Paul, thank you so much. They told me you saved my life. I owe you everything."

Wow, that wasn't the greeting I expected, but I wasn't going to argue. I asked how she was feeling and if she was up to talking. When she nodded in the affirmative, I asked her to continue her story, starting where she had left off.

"Well, as I told you, I saw these two cars on the roof of the parking garage next to my building every day and something was passed between them. When I went down to take a closer look, they chased me and I ended up here. That's about it."

"What can you tell me about the cars? Were they the same vehicles each day?"

"One was always the same, a black Towncar. The other was different each day. They arrived about the same time, around 4:30 in the afternoon."

"Was the bundle passed to or from the Towncar?"

"I saw it go both ways, sometimes from the Lincoln and sometimes to it. That's about all I know, except that I can never repay you for what you did."

If that wasn't an opening line, I never heard one. But being a gentleman, I decided to wait to cherchez la femme until she was at least feeling well enough to eat.

"OK, Grace," I said, "I'll leave you to rest. Don't worry about a thing. There is a police guard at your door, and oh, by the way, have you ever heard of someone named William Francis Smith?"

"William Francis Smith? No, but you will be coming back to see me, won't you?"

"Sure, I'll call again tomorrow. Now get some rest."

I made it an early night. Tomorrow I would be going to meet the famous owner of AB Parking.

William Francis Smith's office was in Library Tower, downtown. It was the tallest building west of the Mississippi. Contrary to popular belief, Los Angeles does have a downtown, with quite a few real skyscrapers; this one was more than 60 stories tall.

One must keep in mind that L.A. started late in the skyscraper business, as technology had to catch up with the concerns over earthquakes. Buildings here are built to sway in a quake. They say the taller ones moved quite a few feet each way at the top during the Northridge quake in 1994. I had been told that if L.A. was ever hit by the "big one," most of the damage would be from desks and filing cabinets flying out the building windows. I'd just as soon be in Texas when that happens.

Smith's offices were on the 17th floor. Most parking companies keep the overhead down with offices in garages or more industrial areas. But not the "owner" of AB Parking.

I handed my card to the receptionist and was shown directly into his office. That seemed strange since I hadn't told them I was coming.

His inner office was huge and laid out like a wealthy men's club. Lots of dark wood and red leather. There had to be a 40-foot distance between the door and the desk, which was the size of a large refrigerator, dropped on its side. He was sitting behind the desk and didn't stand when I came in.

The sight of Smith nearly bowled me over. I thought I had transported into the "Maltese Falcon" and was meeting with Sydney Greenstreet. William Francis Smith weighed 350 pounds, if he weighed an ounce.

"Pardon me for not standing, Mr. Manning. As you can see, I don't stand often. It's getting late in the day; can I offer you a drink—single malt, perhaps?"

I was taken aback by the choice of drink. My dad is a single-malt fanatic. I'm more of a vodka man myself. The fact that Smith offered the whisky told me he may have been expecting Dad and had been prepped for the meeting.

"No thanks. I want to talk about a shooting that seems to be linked to one of the garages your company operates."

"Well," Smith said, "that would be the location on Olympic. My manager told me you were asking questions there the other day. I don't see how AB Parking is connected with any shooting."

"Some gorillas tried to rough me up in the garage but failed. And our client was shot after she saw something strange going on at the garage. There seems to be a connection. Oh, my dad wanted me to ask how Miss LaFlonza is doing these days."

That brought Smith out of his chair. He pushed a button and the door opened. "This interview is over." And I left.

When I got back to the office, Dad, Mom and Jim Walsh were closeted in Dad's office. I walked right in.

"We obviously hit a nerve," Dad was saying. "First, they try to rough up Paulo at the garage, then they cut the brake line on Shirley's car, and now the phone call from Bill Vose at the LAPD."

"What call?" I said.

"Oh, hi, Junior. Bill called and told me the mayor called the chief of police who called the division commander who called Bill and told him to tell us to back off the Grace Lundquist case. Bill knew we wouldn't but had to deliver the message to protect his tail."

"What time did the call come in?"

"About 4:30 p.m."

"Half-an-hour after I mentioned LaFlonza's name to William Francis Smith. He must have friends in high places."

Those words had just left my mouth when the outer office door opened and two men walked in. They identified themselves as members of the state board that licenses private detectives. They told us there had been a number of complaints about our activities and until it was straightened out, they would be pulling all our licenses. For all intents and purposes, Paul Manning and Son Investigations was out of business.

7

The She-Wolf and I Meet Again...

It was obvious Paulo's meeting with William Francis Smith had stepped on some pretty big toes. And they belonged to people not only in City Hall, but also in Sacramento. What the heck was going on here? This was just a friggin' parking lot caper. There couldn't be the kind of money involved that would interest folks at that altitude. Or could there?

I figured it was time to get more information from Betty. She had been in the parking business for 30 years. If anyone knew about parking, it was Betty. When my wife and assistant Shirley returned from making the phone call, she had a funny look on her face.

"Betty wasn't too forthcoming. She sounded frightened. She told me she was very busy and couldn't afford the time to meet with us. I think someone got to her. She did say, however, that perhaps we might want to talk to Marilyn North. She is an auditor and a former parking operator who works out of Seattle. Betty gave me her number. When I called, I found that she's in L.A. working on a job. She'll be here in an hour."

"Wow," I said. "That's a lot in just two phone calls. We have to be careful. We don't want it to look like we are 'investigating' anything. This has to be just a social call. It might be better if we met her at Paulo's. The office may be under surveillance."

"Right, I'll call her back."

I thought it best if just Paulo and I met with North. That way, only our licenses were in jeopardy. Jim Walsh was planning to follow-up with his contacts in the LAPD. I told him to go home and wait. No need for all of us to be at risk of permanent unemployment. Shirley stayed to cover the phones, and discretion being the better, you know the line, I decided I would drive. After the trip down the hill to Cedars-Sinai Medical Center a couple of days ago with Paulo, I didn't want to take any chances.

Paul Junior lived in a small house on a canal in Venice. Yes, there really are canals in Venice, California. In 1904, a developer named Abbot Kinney built a representation of Venice, Italy, on the Southern California coast just south of Santa Monica—complete with canals, bridges and all the accoutrements. Some of the canals were filled in about 1929, but several remain, and small "California bungalows" line the waterways.

Some bungalows are original 1920s; others have been gentrified to multimillion-dollar mansions, with designs ranging from a Hansel and Gretel "witch's house" to chrome, glass and steel. One might wonder how Paulo could afford such a place. It was left to him by my aunt when she passed away a few years ago. One of the original designs, it had the feel of the '20s.

Marilyn North arrived just behind us. She was 50ish, stocky, and in control. She stuck out her hand and introduced herself. "Marilyn North. You must be Paul Manning; who's the kid?" I introduced my son.

"So," she asked, "what do you want to know?"

We sat on Paulo's front porch overlooking the canal. I told her the story and where we were, which was basically nowhere.

"Most people don't understand that parking generates a huge amount of money," North said. "We are talking billions, maybe as much as 20 billion, nationwide. A single location could take in between half a million and a million dollars or more each year. That's room for temptation to step in, plus a lot of room for error. Most parking operators try to do a good job, but the owners drive down their salary, making it difficult to perform. Did you know that the manager of a McDonald's makes six figures, while a parking manager of a location grossing the same amount might make 50K on a good day?

"The other problem is taxes. With so much money floating around, folks want to keep as much as they can," North said. "So they don't report all the income, and thus don't pay the 10% tax. This has two advantages: the obvious one of taking home more, but the other is more subtle. If legitimate operators pay their taxes and an illegitimate one, like your buddy's, William Francis Smith, doesn't, he has a 10% advantage when he bids a job. He can bid it at 10% less and still make the same profit. And we are talking a lot of money here. On one of those million-dollar locations, that's a hundred grand on the bottom line."

"But," I asked, "how can they put so much pressure on the government that my license has been pulled?"

"Well, when you have that much cash, you can spread it around downtown and at the state capital. Smith has his tentacles in a lot of pies, not just parking. It's to his advantage to support the right council members and state legislators. My guess is that with two phone calls, he cut you off at the knees."

"Any idea where we might go from here?"

"I'm auditing one of Smith's locations right now. I'm working for the owner who got suspicious. It's a real mess. The skimming is in six figures, maybe more. Perhaps I can put some pressure on Smith and he'll make a mistake."

"What do you think the guys were doing on the roof of that garage when they were spotted by Grace Lundquist?"

"They were the bagmen for LaFlonza, Smith and his cronies at City Hall. The sacks were filled with cash. My guess is that the garage was a convenient location and they thought it was safe—they just never looked up. They've probably already moved the dropoff."

As we sat there considering what she said, a blonde woman in her late 50s walked up. She was shadowed by two gorillas. She looked very familiar. When she spoke, her accent—like a Sicilian she-wolf—was unmistakable.

"We meet again, Mr. Manning. Your son is a handsome young man, but too young for me. But I digress. No, remain seated; this will take only a minute. You have a choice. Stop what you are doing immediately or you will certainly lose your business, and maybe your lives. I know where you and your beautiful wife live, I know where your son lives, and you know I can deliver." And with that, Maria LaFlonza strode off.

North looked at me with a cold smile. "You sure know how to stir up trouble, don't you, Manning."

8

Is Paul Jr. Falling in Love?

I watched as LaFlonza strolled down the pathway. She was absolutely stunning. I didn't care if she was as old as my mom. And I rather resented the crack about my being too young for her. Dad had her arrested for murder, but she got out early on good behavior. Based on her last few comments, I thought we could now drop the "good."

Dad had his mouth open, but North spoke first. "You got anything to drink around here?" It was my place, so I brought out a bottle of Laphroaig and three glasses. I prefer vodka, but this was a whisky kind of moment. North smiled. "Your kid has good taste, Manning."

"OK," Dad said, after downing two fingers of the malt. "What do you suggest, Marilyn?"

"Like I said, I'm auditing a Smith location. We know he's dirty, but it's tough to get enough on him to put him away. Usually when caught, operators simply pay the amount of the loss to the owner and that's it. Maybe they even keep the location. But there might be another angle.

"The place we are auditing is in the Valley, way out on Ventura Boulevard. I could bring Paul Junior with me and introduce him as my assistant. That would give him cover to sniff around, and maybe he could turn up something more than just lost revenue. At least it would be a start."

"Won't someone recognize me?" I asked. "I have met everyone in the case."

"I don't think so," she said. "This development isn't owned by the same group as your client's employer. Smith never goes there. He likes to keep a close watch on his buddies downtown. It appears they don't switch managers at AB Parking. Once you have a spot, you keep it. So you won't run into your friend from Olympic Boulevard. What do you think, Paul?"

"It's risky," Dad said, "but Paulo can handle himself. I say let's do it."

I had a lump in my throat. My dad didn't hand out compliments too frequently. I love him, but he rarely gushes when it comes to his son. The last time I heard my dad say something positive about me was through a third party. I thought about it and realized that coming from someone else it meant more than from him directly. Parents have a tendency to over-hype their kids. You never know when they mean it. I know my dad means it. And it felt good.

North gave me the Valley address and we agreed I would meet her there at 7 the next morning. She wanted to get started as soon as the garage opened.

I decided to drop by Cedars-Sinai Medical Center to visit our client. Grace Lundquist had come to us with a problem, and before she could say her second sentence, she was hit by a bullet that came through our office window. She was going to be fine, the doctors said, but I had promised to stop in.

When I walked through her open hospital room door, she was sitting up in bed, reading.

"Oh, Paul, thanks so much for coming to see me. I was beginning to think you weren't going to make it." She was beautiful, no doubt about it.

"You are looking great, Grace. How are you feeling?"

"I feel better each day. I know it sounds corny, but having you here helps. Oh, I did remember one thing I forgot to tell you when you dropped by yesterday. One of the bags the goons in those cars were exchanging on the roof of the garage was different. I remembered it because the doctor who came in to see me this morning was carrying one. It was a doctor's bag."

I didn't say a word. My mind was racing. It could be just a coincidence, but Dad had taught me never to believe in coincidences. I was meeting Marilyn North in the morning at the West Valley Medical Center.

Grace and I chatted like old friends. I had seen her at least half a dozen times now and had never touched her, except for the pressure I put on her chest to stop the bleeding when she had been shot.

She reached out and took my hand. I pulled away.

"Grace, you're a client. I must remain professional." I felt like a 15-year-old on his first date.

"Oh, I know, Paul, it's just that you always say the right things and are so nice. I would like to get to know you better."

I was on the ragged edge of ethical suicide. I tried, "Grace, I can't get personally involved with you, at least until the case is over. It would cloud my judgment and wouldn't be right."

I stood up and started for the door. When I reached it, she said: "I knew you would say that. You are right, of course. But the case will be over soon, and I will be out of here."

I looked back, caught a tear in the corner of her eye, and continued out the door. I was Bogie, she was Bergman, but this was L.A., not Paris. The pain in my chest didn't let up until I got to my car.

The drive over the hill to meet Marilyn North was the best Los Angeles has to offer. It was a crisp morning and I took PCH north to Topanga Canyon Road and then over the hill to the West Valley. Since I was going against traffic, the drive was easy. Everyone complains about traffic in Los Angeles, but if you know your way around you can skip the freeways and enjoy the trip. My jeep took the canyon roads like a sports car and the view of the valley from the top of the Santa Monica Mountains was stunning.

Marilyn was in the parking booth when I arrived. She introduced me to the cashier as her assistant and began to explain what we would be doing that day. The manager walked up about then and suggested we go to his office for a cup of coffee. When we entered the office I was stopped cold by an object on his desk, hidden in plain sight, so to speak.

It was black, leather, and looked exactly like the bag Marcus Welby used in his house calls. I began to wonder if Marilyn North and I hadn't stumbled into the center of William Francis Smith's operation.

9

Paul and Bill Hatch a Plan

I left Paul Junior and Marilyn chatting at his house in Venice and decided to check-in with my police buddy, Bill Vose. He had warned me to drop the case, as did the representatives of the licensing board for private investigators, but a friendly drink wouldn't hurt.

Bill worked out of LAPD headquarters at Parker Center downtown. I called him and we agreed to meet halfway between Venice and his office. It would be at Dear John's in Culver City.

Culver City was one of those little towns within the bounds of Los Angeles. It had its own PD, fire department and school system, and the cops didn't take too kindly to strangers driving through late at night. The kids from the local high school had put up a sign at the city limits that read: "You are entering Culver City. Set your clocks back 100 years."

Actually, that's a bit over the top. Culver City is home to a number of movie studios, including Sony Pictures. Sony is on the old MGM lot. All the great movies of the 1930s and '40s put out by Sam Goldwyn and Louis Mayer were made there. On its back lot, Union forces burned Tara in "Gone With The Wind," and the "little people" brought in to play with Dorothy on the Yellow Brick Road trashed the Culver Hotel one wild night in the late '30s.

All over the area are small houses and duplexes where the movie moguls kept their starlets. The locals know where they are. Some of the greatest names in Hollywood got their start on the couches of those duplexes in Culver City.

Dear John's is a bar on Culver Boulevard. It has been there since the late sixties and many stars and studio execs from MGM just up the street have graced his bar to discuss their latest project over a three-martini lunch. Frank Sinatra would play the piano here from time to time during his era.

Bill was sitting at the bar when I arrived. He didn't even say hello. He pointed at a glass of scotch waiting on the bar and said: "You are a pain in the butt, Manning. I told you to lay off this case, and now your kid stirs up one of L.A.'s biggest political contributors. And I hear that Maria LaFlonza, who, I might remind you, has paid her debt to society, isn't too happy either. What's it going to take to call off the Manning boys?"

I got my temper under control, downed about a finger's worth of fine single-malt, and responded: "Listen, Bill, I have had my office shot up, my client is in the hospital, my son assaulted, my PI license suspended, and I've been threatened by that upstanding citizen Maria LaFlonza. And you are telling me to back off? Give me a break."

"What, LaFlonza threatened you? Tell me what happened."

I relayed the story to my best friend, trying not to knock him off his bar stool. Let's face it: I was pissed, I mean really pissed.

"OK, Paul, I understand," Bill said. "But you have to see my side. I have a pension to think of, and if it ever got out that I was covering for you, I'd be writing parking tickets in Pacoima. I do, however, have an idea.

"You say Junior is going to be working with this North woman tomorrow at the West Valley Medical Center. What if we tried a little bait-and-switch? Perhaps we could get your license back if Smith and LaFlonza show their hands."

Bill gave me his plan, and for a flatfoot, it was a good one. At least, it was better than mine, since I didn't have one. I tried to call Paulo, but he was out, probably flirting with our client. I'd catch up with him in the morning.

The next day was absolutely breathtaking. Living in the hills is great; sometimes the marine layer is not too thick and we are above it. Shirley and I sat on the deck with a cup of coffee, watching the city come to life below us.

I thought about Paulo driving over the hills to the Valley. I figured he would be in Topanga or Malibu Canyon and his cellphone wouldn't work till he reached the Valley floor. I would call him and Marilyn then.

Paulo didn't know it yet, but before this day was over, he was going to be in the thick of things.

10

A Simple Plan Gets Complicated

I glanced at Marilyn, who saw the bag, too. I was wondering what to do when my cellphone vibrated. I took the call outside.

"Junior?" It was Dad. He seemed calm, but I could also hear the excitement in his voice. "I've been talking to Bill Vose, and we came up with an idea...."

As he spoke, I could feel a smile forming on my face. The plan was as elegant as it was simple. And if it worked, we would force the players into the open, and Vose could nab them with their hands in the cookie jar—literally.

But before we could put the plan into action, Marilyn and I had work to do. I asked her to step outside and explained what we were going to do. She nodded and went back inside the garage office to proceed with step one: pulling off a rock-solid damning audit of the garage, but we had to work fast.

Finding problems in a parking garage can be easy, as long as you know where to look. I had no clue; however, after years of experience both working in garages and as an auditor, Marilyn knew it all.

Parking garages work mostly in cash, she said, with two basic types of parkers: dailies and monthlies. Plus, she explained, sometimes side deals are cut by the owner of the facility or the operator with local businesses such as restaurants and valet companies.

Dad had told me how he had, nearly three decades ago, with a little help in auditing, discovered a money-laundry operation in a parking facility. Since it's a cash business, the bad guys would simply run dirty money through the garage books and with no records of the actual number of vehicles parking, the cash would suddenly become legitimate.

However, the issues here were different. According to Marilyn, the goal was to under-report the income so the operator didn't have to pay the taxes due. If we could prove that Smith's company was grossly under-reporting the income in the garages, the local DA could go after him and close him down, with substantial jail time. Cities don't like it when you don't pay your taxes.

Dad and Bill's plan went further than just a forensic audit and months of lawyers and courts. They wanted to catch Smith and LaFlonza with the cash in their hot little hands. It was the only way. If Smith could get our licenses pulled in half an hour, he could easily skate on a tax-fraud charge. This had to be iron-clad.

Marilyn and I had to find a way to track the funds from this facility all the way to Smith and LaFlonza. That meant we had to do two things: ensure that money was being siphoned off and into the medical bags, and then "follow the money." If we could find its path from Smith to LaFlonza, then we could catch them in the act.

Dad told me that he figured there was no honor among these thieves and no one trusted anybody, particularly when there was as much cash involved as we had determined earlier. Smith ran 35 locations, Marilyn said, and she estimated that he skimmed about a grand from each location a day. If that was the case, the number was three-quarters of a million dollars a month, in cash. That's a lot of greenbacks to be hauling around.

None of the crooks would trust underlings with such big numbers. Somewhere in the process, Smith and LaFlonza had to meet regularly and divvy it up.

All Marilyn and I had to do was make sure that skimming was occurring, and then I had to follow the cash, discretely, of course, and determine where and when they met to count it. This might take a few days since they probably didn't meet every day. Once we found when and where the exchange was taking place, we would mark some bills, put them in with the regular haul, and then surprise Smith and LaFlonza with the goods. The cops would be waiting and slap on the cuffs. Simple.

Of course, something could go wrong at any point. And in this case, going wrong meant that my neck was on the line. Sounded like fun.

Marilyn had started the audit. Over the last few days, she had counted the cars going in and out, from her vantage point in a parked car across the street. She knew exactly how much money should have been collected on those days. Today, she asked for the reports for those days and guess what, they were off about $500 each day. But that didn't seem like enough.

She then ran a list of active cards on the computerized revenue control system. She compared that with the number listed on the operator's records. There were 575 active cards, but only 385 listed on the books—190 monthly customers at $125 is 23 grand a month. Assuming these were "under the table" deals, and the folks got a discount by paying cash, that made up the difference.

We had our smoking gun. Now all we needed was the location of the transfer.

At about 3 p.m., a car much like the one Lundquist had seen on the roof of the garage showed up, and the garage manager handed the driver the doctor's bag we had seen in the office. It was time for me to jump in the jeep and put my sleuthing skills to good use.

We started up Topanga Canyon, heading for Pacific Coast Highway. Then the car did a strange thing. It turned left on Mulholland. I followed and was so intent on not being spotted that I completely missed the car that was following me. It was open country up there, with no houses, nothing but sagebrush and coyotes.

Then the car in front of me slammed on his brakes. I immediately became aware of the car behind me as it rammed my rear bumper. Suddenly, the whole idea of slapping the cuffs on Smith and LaFlonza didn't seem so simple.

11

I Become a Cavalry of One

Although I had complete faith in Paulo, I was uncomfortable leaving him to follow those mob enforcers. He was well-trained, experienced, and could handle trouble. Still, I was frustrated just sitting there doing nothing while the action was coming down across the hills in the west end of the San Fernando Valley.

Shirley brought me a cup of coffee and must have sensed something was afoot. I told her what Paulo was doing. Her "assistant" hat came off and her "mother" hat went on.

"Well, what the hell are you doing sitting here? Get over there and help him."

But what was I supposed to do? Follow the guy following the bad guys? That made no sense. Should I then call Bill Vose and have him follow me? We could make it a parade. All we would need were trained elephants and it would be perfect. I was muttering into my coffee when the phone rang.

Shirley handed me the phone. It was Vose.

"I thought you'd like to know," he said. "We've been doing a background check on Smith and LaFlonza. There is a connection between the two. Just after LaFlonza got out of jail, about 1995, they formed a company called L and S. As far as we can see, it did only one thing. It bought a piece of land up on Mulholland Drive, between Topanga and the 405 Freeway—about where the paving stops on the Topanga end.

"That's all we could find. There don't seem to be any improvements made on the land, but of course, up there, they could build a skyscraper and the inspectors would never find it."

I told Vose that Shirley was threatening divorce if I didn't drive up to help Paulo. Maybe this way I could be closer to the action. If I was there to look around, I would be only a few minutes from the Medical Center where he and Marilyn were auditing the books. If Paulo got into trouble, he would call, and I could go in with guns blazing.

Vose didn't like the last part, but agreed that it wouldn't hurt to have someone nearby, just in case. "I'll also have a chopper standing by," he said. "It's one of the perks of working at LAPD HQ. I have access to one of the largest nonmilitary air fleets in the country."

The LAPD had recently upgraded with 16 choppers and one twin-engine King Air. Twelve of the helicopters were French Aerospatiale B-2s, four were Bell Jet Rangers and one was a Huey. (There was an uproar when the Frenchies won the contract to upgrade, but the numbers won the day. Not only were they less expensive, but they cost less to run and maintain.) Vose said he could be there if we needed him.

I gave a much-relieved Shirley a kiss and headed for the house. I wanted to trade my car for the corporate four-wheel drive. It was really a 7-year-old Subaru Outback, but better suited for climbing around the dirt roads between the 405 Freeway and Topanga than my Lexus IS 350. The Subaru was my personal car until last year. We had a good year and Shirley insisted.

I took Mulholland west, and in 20 minutes, I was crossing the 405. (Mulholland Drive was named after the engineer, and some say shyster, that brought water from the Owens Valley in the eastern Sierra to turn the desert that was the San Fernando Valley into suburbs for a couple of million people. Of course, Mulholland did pick up a lot of that land on the cheap just before the aqueduct opened. But that's a story for another day.)

As I drove past the mansions west of the 405, I came upon the spot where the pavement ended. No problem, I had my Outback. Well, there was one minor setback—a gate, a locked gate. I was conflicted. Go back the way I had come, or pick the lock and go through?

I had the Subaru. I had my lock picks. No brainer.

The lock took 30 seconds to open. I drove through and closed the gate behind me. The road was packed dirt and the Outback's all-wheel drive took it well. There was little chance of sneaking up on anyone with the cloud of dust I was raising, but I didn't care. I was simply scouting the area, in search of the L and S land, and maybe possible improvements they made.

I rounded a curve and saw a group of cars parked about a quarter of a mile ahead of me. I stopped, pulled out my glasses and checked it out. There were three cars. Two black town cars and in the middle—in the middle was a Jeep that looked exactly like Paulo's.

I crept closer and saw that four rather large men in black dust-covered suits had Paulo braced against the lead car. They slapped what looked like handcuffs on him, put him in the back seat of the car and began to drive directly toward where I was parked.

12

They Throw Me a Curve

I watched helplessly as Paulo was taken from his Jeep, cuffed, and then tossed in the back of a mobmobile. They started up and were driving right toward the spot where I was parked.

I had driven up to Mulholland Drive to check out a lead from my buddy Bill Vose. Parking operator William Francis Smith, a mover and shaker in downtown L.A. politics, and Maria La Flonza, the L.A. rep for some very shady characters from New Jersey, had property up here and could easily have built a shack, or anything they wanted under the building permit department's radar. I also would be in the area if Paulo needed assistance with his "follow-the-money" assignment.

I was right about the need for assistance, and maybe I would find the hideout by taking over for my son and following that car. I moved my Outback behind some boulders and waited for them to pass. I then followed from about half a mile back. No need to alert them too soon of their impending doom. Or so I hoped.

They slowed then turned into a canyon. According to the Ordinance survey map I'd brought, there was no exit. I decided to follow the rest of the way on foot.

Most people think that L.A. is this big urban blight with 12 million people covering all the land from Santa Barbara to San Jan Capistrano and inland to San Bernardino. It's not really like that. There are large tracts of land as wild and rough as you will find anywhere. This part of the Santa Monica Mountains between Malibu and the San Fernando Valley was one of them.

It's populated with deer, puma, coyotes, snakes, hawks, eagles and every type of rabbit, squirrel, rat and other vermin you could name. The road isn't paved. And there's not a house around for miles. It was a perfect place for a hideout.

I called Cmdr. Bill Vose at the LAPD and told him what was up. Vose said he would be standing by with SWAT and a couple of helicopters from the city fleet. We decided that I would reconnoiter and then get back to him so we could devise a plan.

The road curved to the right, and I could see trees over the ridge. I rounded the bend and got a big surprise. Shack? Yeah, right. I should have known folks like LaFlonza and Smith wouldn't pinch pennies.

This place was huge—7,500 square feet, if a foot. There were split levels, a swimming pool, a four-car garage, tennis courts, and from what I could see, a lawn out back the size of a nine-hole golf course. It was all done up in Spanish tile and white stucco. A real hacienda.

The car with Paulo had just stopped when I caught sight of the house. Paulo was dragged out of the car and around to the side. They took him down some stairs, opened a door, tossed him inside and locked the door not only with the deadbolt secured on the door, but also with a padlock, and then came back around to the front and disappeared inside.

They seemed to have little fear of his escaping, as they left no guard on the door.

I watched the place for a few minutes; no one was coming or going. I did notice that the power was supplied from a generator in an enclosure about 100 yards off. It was completely self-contained.

I called Bill. "We're ready to move," he said. "Did you see Paul?"

"Yes," I told him. "He looked OK." I described the layout. I heard him whistle over the phone.

"Wow, those folks really know how to make things happen without a trace of city involvement. There is no record of any building in that entire area. That means we can't get floor plans and figure out where they are keeping him."

I told him it was obvious where Paul was being held and, in fact, fairly easy to get him out. I thought they didn't have much electronic security in the way of CCTV or motion detectors. These wise guys must have considered the location, and that no one knew where it was, sufficient security.

As Bill was considering the logistics, I looked up and saw a very large gentleman in a dark suit carrying a rifle ambling in my direction. I hit the ground and hung up the phone. I was fairly sure I hadn't been spotted as he seemed to be simply walking the perimeter of the property. I guess this also provided security. My son's rescue wasn't going to be as easy as I had thought.

I walked quietly back down the side of the road and found a position out of sight where I could view the access road. I called Bill and filled him in.

"Well, perhaps we have a good chance of catching Smith and LaFlonza. If we leave Paul there, he is probably OK for the time being. The men we have following Smith report that he is being driven in your general direction. We don't know where LaFlonza is, but my guess is she's headed there, too. It's their opportunity to resolve the Manning situation."

That's what I was afraid of. The "resolution" of the Manning situation certainly didn't bode well for Paulo.

Bill and I agreed that he would stage SWAT in a nearby canyon so as not to alert the goons in the house. I was to keep an eye out for any new arrivals.

An hour passed and I was tired and hungry. In my plans for this trek, I hadn't figured I would be this far from a McDonald's. Then I spotted a large car winding up the road. It was Smith, with someone else in the car. I decided to circle around and maneuver closer to the house.

When the car stopped, the driver opened the door. Smith hoisted his 300 pounds out of the back seat. He then turned around and put his hand out to assist the other person from the car.

When I saw who it was, my mind went wild. How could she be here, but apparently not under duress? I could tell because she gave Smith a peck on the cheek and put her arm through his as they sauntered to the front door.

What the hell was going on?

13

I HAD BEEN WRONG FOR 30 YEARS

My mind was reeling. This was all wrong. It couldn't be happening. Over thirty years ago I got my start in the detective business by saving a girl from the gas chamber and having a treacherous mob boss jailed for the crime. That girl was an innocent from Iowa who had worked in a garage where the murder took place.

I put Maria LaFlonza (with the help of the LAPD) in jail for the murder of Gilberto Quintana. She didn't get much time because it was a "crime of passion." She had returned to LA and resumed her place as head of the LA mob.

My client at the time, Betty Beeson, through my good offices, got her start as the co-owner of a parking company and was now head of one of the largest operations in the city. She was also cozying up to one of the biggest scumbags in town. I had to think about this.

The best thing to do was get out of there, meet up with Bill Vose, and regroup.

Vose and SWAT had set up a base camp a couple of ridges over. It was a short walk. I guess I looked shaken when I arrived.

"Is everything OK, any word on Paul?" he asked.

"No, no change. I'm sure he's still OK in the basement of the house. There is another complication. Smith arrived, and he has a guest, Betty Beeson."

"What, he kidnapped her too?"

"No, she wasn't kidnapped. She held his hand and kissed him on the cheek."

"That makes no sense," responded Bill. "She hates Smith. He's her biggest competitor. Why would she be friendly now, after all these years?"

I had to mull it over. Something didn't make sense. LaFlonza and undoubtedly Smith had come within a hair's breadth of pinning a murder on Betty. When LaFLonza thought she was going to get away with it (and kill me), she told the story that she had killed Quintana in a lover's quarrel. It was only because Jim Walsh had showed up a few minutes earlier, heard the whole thing, and saved the day (and my life) that she didn't get away with it.

LaFLonza was the LA representative of some pretty shady characters from New Jersey. She was also a Grade-B actress and for all we knew, was one of Howard Hughes' mistresses. When we caught her she was living in a mansion owned by Hughes' studio.

I had always figured Betty was in the wrong place at the wrong time. She was a good patsy. I did think her story about Gilberto tripping on a rubber plant and her discovering a laundering operation at the garage was a little thin, but attributed that to her young age. The fact that she was blonde and beautiful might have clouded my judgment.

Plus, Betty had recommended auditor Marilyn North who had helped us get the goods on Smith. Why would she have turned him in if they were in business together? It made no sense at all.

All that aside, I knew we still had a problem. Paul was being held by these cretins. We had to get him out. Once he was safe, we could deal with Smith and his crew.

I told Bill that the safest way to extricate Paul was to do it on the quiet. I assumed there were only two guards. If we could distract them, we could grab Paul and get out.

Bill wanted to storm the place and arrest everyone in sight. I reminded him that if we did that we might have a couple of Smiths gunsels on kidnapping, but all Smith had to do was deny, deny, deny, and he would be back in business. Plus LaFlonza hadn't showed up yet.

If we could make Smith believe that Paul escaped we could keep our investigation on course.

Bill wasn't happy but he agreed to try it my way.

A patrol car would start down the road to the house. Hopefully the guards would stop it and they could chat for a while. While they were so engaged, I would go down to the entry to the basement, which fortunately was outside, free Paul, and hightail it out of there.

It was amazing. When the patrol car cruised down to Smith's house, the two guards walked over and blocked it. The cops told them that they were looking for the driver of a car they'd found abandoned up the road (Paul's) and asked if they had seen anything. They had instant memory loss. The conversation continued for a few minutes, after moving on to the Dodgers and their prospects, and then the cops left.

That gave me enough time to get to the basement door. I picked the locks, got Paul, and relocked the door. These idiots would think he teleported himself out of the room.

Paul was fine but angry. He let himself be suckered by these wise guys and wanted revenge. I told him there would be time enough for that later.

After we downed some grub at the police base camp, we decided to go back to watch the house.

The next arrival didn't surprise me much. It was LaFlonza, and Marilyn North was with her. They were pretty chummy, too. I wondered if that was how LaFLonza knew exactly where we were when she accosted us at Paul's house in the Venice Canals.

Just then, one of the gunsels when to check on Paul. About 30 seconds later everyone was in front of the house and Betty was screaming her head off. She wasn't frightened, she was angry.

"What kind of incompetents do you employ, William. And you, Maria. How can you let these Manning guys continue to give you the slip?" She was mad as hell.

It was like they all worked for her.

Then the fog began to lift. I had been wrong about a lot of things. I had been wrong for 30 years....

14

Adding Insult to Injury

It came into focus so rapidly my head whipped around and I looked directly at Paulo. My son gave me a shrug. "What?" he said.

"I have been conned from the very beginning. In that first case before you were born, Betty killed Quintana and for some reason LaFlonza took the fall. You saw the way they were talking down there; it was as if Betty were the boss. Betty—the boss?"

That was it. Betty Beeson was somehow connected with the New Jersey group, and my guess was that if we did a little research, we would find that the only time she had been in Iowa was when the train bringing her to California crossed the cornfields.

OK, now what? I was sure I was right, but how to prove it? My guess was that Betty called me that morning 30 years ago in fear. She had killed a man and needed help. She made up a story, which was shaky, but it got me involved. However, before I could get to her, LaFlonza had stepped in and started to clean up the mess. Unfortunately, I kept stirring things up, and the problem wasn't going away. Betty must be connected for LaFlonza to have gone to prison for her.

I turned to Bill and told him my scenario.

"Powerful enough mob ties for LaFlonza to have risked the gas chamber?"

"Not really," I said. "She had the best lawyers money could buy. She knew that with a 'crime of passion' defense she would get only a few years, plus time off for good behavior. For all we know, the judge was on the take, too."

"Well, it's pretty far-fetched. Betty would have to be somebody's daughter, or have some other family relation. And I don't think so, with a name like Beeson."

That was it. Bill had nailed it. Betty was the daughter of some capi di capos Back East. She probably came out here to get a feel for the family business and got herself in trouble. As for her name, she changed it so she could operate in the open. She had been running the wiseguy operation here in L.A. for the past 30 years. But Bill was skeptical.

"Sure, it's a theory, and I may even believe it, but we have this problem. Evidence. Seeing her with Smith and hearing her say a few words on the front porch wouldn't constitute a case for the D.A. At this point, we got nothing. I'm sending SWAT home, and my suggestion is that you two go soak that Santa Monica Mountain dirt off in a long, hot bath."

Paulo and I got into the Outback and headed back to the office. To say Shirley was relieved was an understatement. First she hugged us both and then she socked me on the arm. "Why did you let him get into this mess?"

Paulo and I spoke at the same time. When the dust settled, we all agreed that perhaps we needed to be more careful in the future. Dealing with the crooked-nose group wasn't the same as chasing down payment skips and snapping a few incriminating photos through a bedroom window.

One thing was certain. Betty, LaFlonza and Smith weren't going away. But we had an advantage: They didn't know what we knew. They hadn't seen me at the hideout in the mountains and may have figured that even if I were around, I was too busy rescuing Paulo and wouldn't have taken note of Betty and Marilyn.

Maybe we could use that to our advantage. We decided to call it a day.

I asked Paulo to join us for dinner, but he said he wanted to drop by Cedars-Sinai to see how our current client, Grace Lundquist, was faring. She and Paulo were becoming close. Paulo was trying, and failing, to maintain an ethical distance with the young, beautiful client. I wasn't worried. She seemed like a nice girl, and Paulo's ethics would stand up to anyone's.

I was looking forward to having an evening alone with my wife. We arrived at the house off Mulholland Drive and all was quiet. Not a car around, nor sign of tampering with the door.

For the first time in almost 24 hours, I began to relax. That lasted about 10 seconds.

We walked into the living room and found Betty Beeson, Maria LaFlonza, William Francis Smith and Marilyn North had made themselves comfortable. To add insult to injury, Smith was drinking some of my 15-year-old Laphroaig. Betty was holding a very lethal-looking automatic.

"Hello Paul, Shirley," Betty said. "I have decided that it's time to bring this chapter in our lives to a close, once and for all."

15

LAUREL AND HARDY...NOT

"What a fine kettle of fish you have gotten us into this time, Stanley." Except I was Ollie.

Betty had completely snookered me. I glanced at Shirley and she was looking back with an expression of "I told you so." The problem was, she didn't really have any reason to complain about Betty. In fact, it was Shirley who had recommended my services back when she ran the building where Betty was the night parking manager.

OK, now that I had figured out this wasn't all my fault, it was time to do something about it.

"Well, Betty, or whatever your name is, what do you want? If it's me, fine, but let Shirley go. She's not involved in any of this." Yeah, right, like Beeson was going to buy that, but at least it would give us time.

"You know, Paul, I really liked you in the beginning, and still do even now," she said. "You are certainly persistent, and you do solve cases. I guess you are smart, too. But this just can't continue. I have responsibilities, employees, a business to run. I simply can't have you interfering in my affairs.

"You have probably determined that I am not exactly who I said I was. I was sent out by my uncle to check up on the business here in Los Angeles. I was here to get a job with the parking company, take notes and report back. No big deal. It was his way of introducing me to the family operation.

"I had an affair with Gilberto," she said, "and then he got possessive. I tried to break it off and he wouldn't take no for an answer. The day he died, I was fighting him off and he hit me.

I picked up a knife and stabbed him. I knew I was in trouble, so I called Shirley and she told me to call you.

"When I calmed down, I realized that Uncle Mario could handle the problem and called him. He told me what to do and got Maria involved," she said. "You thought the notes I was sending to my uncle were to expose a scam with the garage. They were just there to confirm the numbers Maria was reporting each week.

"Maria and I cooked up the plan between the time I called you and when you arrived at the parking garage. I waited until I saw you, screamed and ran out the back door. You thought the death had just occurred, but I stabbed him a couple of hours earlier. Then Maria took over and you fell for it. It was like reeling in a fish. You love beautiful blondes. Look who you married."

At that point, Shirley had taken all she could stand and started to rush across the room at Betty. I grabbed her as Beeson pointed the automatic at Shirley's heart and begin to squeeze the trigger. "I might as well shoot her now as later."

"Wait!" It was LaFlonza. "We still have to be certain we won't be connected with their deaths. We can't kill them here, unless we're forced to. We should take them out to the house in the hills and make them simply disappear. We have too much riding on this to bring attention on us."

Beeson released the pressure on the trigger, and I started breathing again. One crisis over. Someone once told me that you solve problems one at a time. If you are in a seven-story building and trapped by a fire that is about to burn you to death, you jump out the window. Once out the window, you then have a few seconds to solve the second problem you just created. At this point, we were heading directly toward that window.

Smith was smiling and sipping my Laphroaig. What a rat.

Marilyn North looked worried. She was an auditor, and a tough woman. But I don't think she had the stomach for this. She said to Beeson, "I'd better leave. You don't want me too close to this if you are going to use me in the future."

I got the feeling that she may have just switched sides. So did Beeson.

"Marilyn, why don't you go over and stand with Shirley. I've had my doubts about you for some time. Perhaps we should clean house."

Smith continued to smile as Marilyn, shaken, walked over to Shirley.

"You know, Paul, the idea of my working undercover proved providential, and it came from something you did 30 years ago. You put me together with DC McGuire, and he taught me the parking business. He told me I was good at it. He was right.

"I kept my cover and was able to move freely within the L.A. business community. My life would have been much more difficult here without that knowledge. I guess I do owe you some thanks."

I was beginning to prefer the she-wolf LaFlonza. At least with her you knew where you stood. But what to do now?

LaFlonza and Smith were brandishing weapons and herding us toward the door.

"We'll go in your car, Paul. We can drop it off later."

We needed the cavalry, and I didn't hear any bugles.

16

Does It End Just Like Chinatown?

Grace was sitting at a table in her hospital room eating dinner. Even in her hospital gown and robe, she was stunning. No doubt about it. I was smitten and smitten hard.

My goal was to remain professional until we had solved the case, and then properly "court" the wonderful Grace Lundquist. I stood silently at the open door and just gazed at her.

"Oh, Paul, I wasn't expecting you until later. The doctor told me that if I promise to rest, I could go home tomorrow. They just don't keep you as long in the hospital as they used to."

Her smile melted my heart. It took every ounce of self-control to keep from rushing to her side and grabbing her hand. Damn ethics. I hoped she understood. She asked me to sit with her. I still hadn't said a word.

"What's happened? Is everything OK?"

I finally found my tongue and told her about my problem in the mountains and how Betty Beeson was now our prime suspect.

"Do you mean she ran the entire operation? It seems incredible. I guess it's not only who you know, but who your uncle is that counts."

I sat for a few more minutes and enjoyed her presence. Grace Lundquist was going to see a lot more of Paul Manning Jr., there was no doubt about that. She told me she was tired, and I helped her back into bed.

"Paul," she said as I turned to leave, "I know you can't say anything now, but you should know that I am falling for you."

This may not be Paris, and I may not be Bogie, she may not be Bergman, but I knew at that moment that this story was going to have a very different ending than the one so many years ago on that airstrip in Casablanca.

When I got to my car, I realized that I had left my cellphone in Dad's Outback. I didn't want to be far from a phone, particularly with all that had been happening. I drove up Nichols Canyon to Mulholland Drive and turned right at my parents' house.

Then I recognized Mom's SUV heading toward me. As it passed, I saw it was full of people. Dad was driving. I caught only a glimpse of him, but he didn't appear happy. Something was up. I decided to "follow that car" and check it out.

They stayed on Mulholland and drove due west. Past Laurel Canyon, Benedict Canyon and the "Casiano" gate for Bel Air. We then drove over the 405 and past the Skirball Center. Five minutes later, they stopped at a gate that marked the end of the paved road. I had turned off my lights as soon as we passed the freeway and was hanging back.

A woman got out of the back seat, then unlocked and opened the gate. She got back in, but it was into the driver's seat, and they drove off. It seemed strange, but Mom's SUV had a bench front seat. All three of them must have been sitting in the front. She didn't stop and close the gate.

I followed. There was no question as to their destination. They were headed for Smith's palatial hideout where I had been held captive only a few hours before.

I had a choice. I could follow or I could call for reinforcements. Since I knew where they were going, the latter seemed the better decision. I turned around, went to the gas station near the 405 and called Commander Bill Vose of the LAPD.

I filled him in and we agreed to meet in the same canyon that had been the staging area earlier in the day when they were preparing to rescue me. Then I headed back to Smith's hideout.

That part of Mulholland Drive was tricky. It was as dark as any unused road, and rough and narrow. There were 100-foot cliffs on either side of the road. It was slow-going both for whoever was driving the SUV and for me, but my sure-footed Jeep was able to make up the distance I had lost calling the LAPD. I caught sight of the SUV's lights about 500 feet ahead.

They seemed to be swerving back and forth and picking up speed. What the hell was she doing, trying to get them all killed?

Then, as if someone had thrown a switch, the SUV's lights disappeared. I hit the brakes and heard a shot, and then the blaring of a horn cut through the night.

17

And So It Ends...

They say your life flashes before your eyes just before you die. I've always wondered how they knew that. Think about it.

I'm Paul Manning, and I've been a PI in L.A. for more than four decades. I've seen the city change and grow. I've lived through fires, floods, earthquakes, riots and even the odd Academy Award ceremony. This is a great city, a vibrant city, a true citadel of the world. It's also a great place to cruise, to see the sights.

Take a drive down Sunset to the sea, or up PCH (that's Pacific Coast Highway) to Malibu. Drive down La Cienega or up Melrose. Spend the afternoon at the Third Street Promenade in Santa Monica or have a leisurely lunch at the Cheesecake Factory in the Marina. You can shop in Beverly Hills, or at the Grove. You can eat at the Farmers Market and take your kids to nearby Disneyland, Knott's or Universal.

You can immerse yourself in any culture you choose, whether it's Chinese, Jewish, Vietnamese, Mexican or Russian. We have Persians (that's what they call themselves here), Ethiopians, Japanese, Koreans and, yes, even a Canadian or two, particularly in the winter. This is the most international city on earth. And it's exhilarating.

Unless you happen to be riding down Mulholland Drive at 9 p.m., with a gun lodged in your neck, certain that at the end of the drive, you and your wife are going to be shot. How I got to this point in the road turns the tale.

My son, Paul—he's my partner in the detecting business—and I were interviewing a new client, Grace Lundquist, when she was shot. Paulo saved her life and was quickly becoming romantically involved with the beautiful blonde.

Her shooting led us to the parking business, and a crooked operator who was in cahoots with some rather shady characters from New Jersey.

It started nearly 40 years ago when I put a mob boss in jail. She was a B-grade actress named Maria LaFlonza and went to prison for murder. She was released on good behavior and back in business. Her current partner was a creep named William Francis Smith.

Paulo and I tripped over them while we were looking for the gunsel who broke the window of my office in the process of shooting Grace. Smith was a wheeler-dealer in politics downtown and had caused our PI licenses to be revoked. We were operating without a net.

While rescuing Paulo, who had been kidnapped by these two cretins, I got the surprise of my life. My original client in that first case years ago, Betty Beeson, turned out to be the niece of a mob boss from Back East, and was running the entire L.A. operation. I was had, and had good.

Betty was holding the gun pressed into my neck. The other passengers were my wife, Shirley; LaFlonza; Smith' and Marilyn North, an auditor who seemed to be on the up-and-up, but ...

Shirley and I had been waylaid at our home in the Hollywood Hills and were being "taken for a ride." Betty meant business. Her words before we got into the car: "I think it's time to end this chapter in our lives once and for all." And I had no doubt what that meant.

We were heading to Smith's luxurious hideout in the Santa Monica Mountains off Mulholland Drive above Woodland Hills. I was driving, with Betty seated behind me holding the gun. Shirley was next to me in the front seat. LaFlonza and Smith were in the second row of seats next to Betty; Smith had a gun on North, who was in the jump-seat at the back. The jury was out as to whose side she was on. Based on the situation, I expected her to side with whoever didn't shoot her.

Betty was getting more and more wired as we neared Smith mansion. She talked tough, but her lieutenants likely did the dirty work. I doubted she'd ever pulled the trigger.

"Come on, Paul, hit the gas," Betty said. "Let's get this over with. Maria, when we get there, you and William take them out back and finish the job. I'll call my assistants, and they can clean up afterwards."

I was looking for a way out but didn't see one.

"Paul, you have been meddling in my life since the early '60s," Betty said. "I can't have you continuing to upset my business. My uncle expects me to take action, and I know how he wants problems like you solved."

The pressure of what was about to happen was having an effect. Betty wasn't accustomed to having blood on her hands. LaFLonza and Smith did it all. Betty had been the contact with the East Coast. I thought if I could use that to my advantage...

"Three murders and you get off scot-free," I told her. "And if something goes wrong, Maria will take the fall like she did last time. Must be nice, Maria, forced to live with that. You are second-rate as an actress and now you play second-fiddle to Betty."

"Shut up, Paul!" Betty screamed. "Just drive."

We had reached the gate that led to the dirt portion of Mulholland Drive and Smith's hideout. Betty got out and unlocked and opened the gate. Then she opened the driver's-side door and told me to move over. She would drive.

"Keep a gun on Paul, William. If he so much as twitches, shoot him, and Shirley, too."

Betty was out of control. We were taking the dirt road far too fast. I buckled my seat belt and made sure Shirley did, too.

As we neared the mansion, Maria said in a low voice: "You wouldn't make me take another fall, would you, Betty? I don't want to go back to prison."

"Shut up," Betty said. "You were well-compensated for your little vacation. We'll provide for you, whatever happens."

A minute later, I was deafened by a shot that sounded as if it had come from a gun six inches from my ear. The SUV started to careen toward a drop-off straight ahead.

The last thing I remembered was another shot. Fade to black.

When I came to, I was deafened by the SUV's horn. Betty was draped across the driver's airbag and pressing against the horn. We had gone over a low cliff and slammed into a dirt berm. Everyone was out cold—Betty was the coldest. There was a bullet wound to her temple. Nothing to be done there. The second "shot" turned out to be the airbags inflating.

I checked Shirley and she was breathing. As I turned to check out the gang in the back, the passenger door was jerked open. There was Paulo.

"Dad, Mom, you OK?"

"We're fine. Check the back seats and take the guns from Smith and LaFlonza."

I pulled Betty off the horn. The silence was welcome relief.

Shirley began to stir and told me she was OK. We left Betty where she was, and we climbed out. Paul had the passengers in the back under control. At that moment, the cavalry arrived. Bill Vose and the LAPD SWAT unit had been notified by Paulo and were all over the scene.

But what happened? Who shot Betty Beeson?

Did Smith see an opportunity to take over the operation? Had LaFlonza just had too much? Did North change sides and grab a gun? But why pick that moment? It was a desperate move. We all could have been killed. Paulo wasn't too careful when he took the guns from the dazed duo in the back, and we didn't know which gun belonged to whom.

I caught LaFlonza's eye as they put her in the back of a black-and-white. They flashed determination, but also a steely glint. She fixed her sights on me for just a moment, but it was enough.

The next afternoon, we were sitting on Paulo's front deck. The Venice canals were beautiful. The sun was perfect. Just another day in paradise.

Grace was holding Paulo's hand, and it looked as if she wasn't going to let go. Bill and I each had a glass of 18-year-old Laphroaig, and Shirley was nursing her chardonnay.

"They have clammed up," Bill said. "No one will say anything. Lawyers everywhere. I'm not certain we will ever sort out who shot Betty."

"I don't think that's important, "I said. "They will all go down for the count."

There was a buzzing on the table. It was Paulo's cell. He answered. After listening a few minutes, he smiled and shot me a look. Manning and Son Investigations was back in business. I wondered if it was a blonde.

Acknowledgments

If you enjoyed the first installment of *Death by Parking*, you can thank Mrs. Garfield, my eighth-grade English teacher who told me just to start writing and see what comes out; Mrs. Albright, my tenth-grade English teacher who said when I complained of writer's block, "Suck it up and start writing anything;" my father, who told me to write about what I know (the locations in *Death* are places I know); a bistro owner in Ottawa who taught me the wonders of single malt whisky; Winston Churchill who hated the rule about dangling participles ("It's a rule up with which I will not put"); Sergey Bren and Larry Page who put so many researchers out of business with the wonders of Google (how else could I know about Paul's convertible or his side arm), but more to the point, thanks to Carla Green and the folks at Clarity Designworks, who got me off my duff and pulled the first three episodes into a book and gave invaluable editing help, most of which I took after I learned to take my own advice and remember that words are not sacrosanct and fewer is always better: and of course, Amazon, who has made self-publishing a low-cost reality. If you grace me by reading this book, I don't care if it's on paper, on your laptop, iPad, your smart phone or Kindle. It's the content that counts, not the medium. I must thank my wife, Robyn, for her infinite patience in all things JVH, and the support of friends Shelly, Astrid, Mike, David, and Ted. It's nice to know there are people who will bail you out and not ask too many questions.

About the Author

JVH is John Van Horn, Founder, Editor, and Publisher of *Parking Today Magazine*. He has spent more than 40 years working in the parking industry, first as head of sales for an international manufacturer of parking equipment, and then as the head of the most widely read business to business publication in that industry. He has spoken before parking groups on six continents, helped in the formation of a number of parking organizations, and hopefully made a small impact on that niche within a niche industry. He graduated from UCLA, served in the Army during the Vietnam era, and lives with his wife Robyn, dog Suki and cat Brackets in Los Angeles.

Made in the USA
Lexington, KY
26 February 2018